Because Sometimes Something _Extraordinary_ Happens

Because Sometimes Something Extraordinary Happens

A Collection of Winning Short Stories

Debz Hobbs-Wyatt

Bridge House

© Copyright 2019
Debz Hobbs-Wyatt
The right of Debz Hobbs-Wyatt to be identified as author of this work has been asserted by her in accordance with the Copyright, Designs and Patents Act 1988

All rights reserved

No parts of this publication may be reproduced, stored in a retrieval system, or transmitted in any form or by any means, electronic, mechanical, photocopying, recording or otherwise without prior permission of the copyright owner.

British Library Cataloguing in Publication Data
A Record of this Publication is available from the British Library

ISBN 978-1-907335-69-3

This edition published 2019 by Bridge House Publishing
Manchester, England

Cover photos:

> Bottom left: photograph of the author © Rose Steward Photography
> *Instagram @rosephotography211*
>
> Top right: photograph of the author's nan taken in Hove 1937.

All Bridge House books are published on paper derived from sustainable resources.

*Dedicated to my grandparents
Ted and Alice Wyatt and Alfred and Elsie Sheldrake*

Contents

Learning to Fly 11
Mirror Image 18
Chutney 31
We Went There 48
I am Wolf 60
Graffiti 82
The Red Queen 89
Rats in the Attic 106
Thinking in Circles 116
Director's Cut 124
The Theory of Circles 141
Because Sometimes Something Happens 158
When the Bees Die 169
Four Minutes in April 183
Paper Chains 187
Jigsaw 199
Goldfish Parade 213
About the Author 243

Preface

Focus on short stories a friend once told me. This was as I started working on my second novel, while still collecting rejections from the first. But people like novels, I said. Movies are made from novels, I said. People read novels more than short stories, I said. The advice was given to me by a colleague (I was a scientist at the time) and was a remark made in jest, but I soon came to realise that he *was* actually right. I needed to learn, I needed to develop as a writer and a novel is like *running before you can walk*.

I had written short stories before, but I now started to look closely at it as an art form, and I quickly fell in love with the short story for what it can do. I admire writers like: Jon McGregor (a real favourite), Alice Munroe, George Sanderson, Lisa Blower... Marc Haddon has a great short story collection; Stephen King has written some amazing short stories.

It is said that the novel is a tour of the whole house, while the short story is a glimpse through a window. You have to learn to be sharp, succinct, considered in your choice of word. Make everything feel as if it's the perfect word in the right place. And what's more, with skill, as all these writers have, you can create love, empathy, fear, hope... you can change mood; make a reader laugh, cry, and smile with very few words. And that gift is one I admire and would read their stories in awe and think: *Wow. If I was half that good...*

My very first short story success came while I was working on a novel, and the first lines of the story were in my head when I woke one morning, whispering to me over and over in a child's voice as if I was possessed. I knew it was a story begging for life. It turned out to be the story, *Jigsaw*, that was later selected by Bridge House Publishing and chosen as the lead story, inspiring the cover artwork of their first ever anthology. Who knew? After that, I chose to let the novel rest a while to work on my craft. I am still learning because nothing is ever perfect – just as perfect as it can be right now. I spent at least a couple of years writing only short stories and submitting them to all kinds of competitions and anthologies and I was amazed when I started to have success. In fact, while I write fewer short stories now, I have had success with at least one short story being published every year since that first one in 2008 with over thirty successes overall. What I also found was not only did my writing develop while I experimented with new styles and voices, but that some of the stories formed a blueprint for development into novels. My first and, to date, only published novel (hopefully that will not be the case for too much longer) *While No One Was Watching* started life as a short story. The novel was published by Parthian Books in 2013.

Never underestimate the power of the short story. I have to thank Gill James at Bridge House Publishing for taking a chance on me when she accepted *Jigsaw* back in 2008. She later published several other stories of mine before she eventually took me on to work alongside her, first in marketing, and later in selecting and editing short stories – I learned so much from her. But also I must give thanks to her for allowing me to publish this collection. It's a volume of work spanning over a decade – some previously published stories, some competition winners, lots of runners-up and one or two brand new ones. I have selected a variety of stories that I think are diverse enough to make an interesting read. Although as I read them together I see similarities in themes, a lot of exploring grief and broken minds but I like to think with some humour as well. I use a mix of adult voices and children's voices, a touch of darkness and danger.

While I like to think of them as exploring what it is to be human – what I really wanted to show was ordinary people when something extraordinary happens.

I hope you enjoy what you read and I give thanks to the masters of short story writing who inspired me on this journey and continue to inspire me every day.

Learning to Fly

My brother always cried when he watched TV movies.

"I thought scousers were supposed to be 'ard," I told him.

"Everyone's got a sensitive side, Jen."

"Not me," I said.

"Even tomboys are allowed to cry."

"Yeah, whatever," I said.

It was my brother that found the blackbird's nest that spring. It was my brother that taught me to believe in happy ever after. And it was my brother that was killed in Afghanistan.

We found out on a Wednesday. It was raining. Mum said the rain meant something. Yeah, it meant the washing was wet on the line. It meant the blackbirds didn't fledge. And it meant I was never gonna see our Robert again or make fun of his bright orange cagoule.

Dad was standing in the doorway holding a plastic milk bottle and saying all we needed was another cup of tea, like that would bring him back; like that would make everything alright.

"I don't want any more tea," Mum said.

"Nor do I," Nan said. Then she said, "People always do that."

"Do what?" Dad said.

"Make tea."

"Who?"

"On the telly. When someone dies they always make tea."

"Oh," Dad said.

And then he just stood there fiddling with the green lid of the milk bottle and looking at me. So I said, "Go on then,

I'll 'ave another brew" even though I never wanted one. But I didn't know what I was supposed to do. I didn't know anyone that had died before, not really. Floss died, our dog, but that was different, she was old and she died in her sleep. That's how I want to go. I don't want to be blown up by a bomb in Afghanistan.

It went quiet for a bit when Dad made the tea, we heard him clinking a spoon and it was ages before he came back in. When he did he looked like he'd been chopping onions again. Mum looked up then and said, "I knew." She was sitting at the table looking down at her hands, holding a photograph of our Robert. "I dreamed about it last night."

"Don't be daft," Dad said.

"I did," she said. "I dreamed our Robert was standing by the bed telling me he had to go. He was with Grandad Harry."

"But Grandad Harry's not dead," I said.

"I know," she said. Then she added, "Best give him a ring to make sure."

"I wish 'e *was* dead," Nan said and she got that look when she thinks about the trollop from the chippy – the one Grandad ran off with.

"He was there," Mum said. "I'm telling you, he was *really* there, stood at the bottom of the bed."

"Shut up," Dad said.

They buried Robert in a box with a flag draped across it, while some fella played the trumpet, only Dad said it wasn't a trumpet, it was a bugle. I told him I didn't care what it was.

"It's to do with the shape of the bell," Dad said. "A bugle is conical."

"Conical? How can a bugle be funny?"

Nothing about that day was funny.

"Anyway, what does it matter?" I said. "What does any of it matter?"

"Everything matters," Mum said. Then she sat in the dark and cried.

And Dad got drunk.

And Nan said she would stay with us for a bit, until we felt better but Mum said we'd never feel better. So Nan sat in the dark and cried too. And she said it was a pity Grandad Harry *wasn't* dead and then she started talking about the trollop again. That's when I went outside to see the blackbirds because I promised our Robert I'd look out for them.

But I was too late. The blackbirds were gone.

Our blackbirds had all left while some fella in a poxy uniform played the bloody trumpet. I felt **CRAP.** Crap in bold and underlined. Only really I felt worse but I couldn't think of a word for worse.

"It's not fair," I said. I said it out loud, in the garden with no shoes on and wet grass between me toes. I said it as I looked up at our Robert's bedroom window, where we used to watch the blackbirds making their nest. And I said it to God, not that I believed in God anymore. What kind of God lets people like our Robert get killed? Mum says it's not God's fault, she says it's the Prime Minister's. But it's too late now. I hate God and I hate the Prime Minister.

"It's not fair," I said. "None of it's fair."

I don't know if I meant about the Prime Minister, not seeing the blackbirds fledge or our Robert getting killed in Afghanistan.

It all felt the same.

My brother said the Latin name for the blackbird is *Turdus merula*. I laughed. "It can't be," I said. "Turd? You're making it up."

But he wasn't.

Robert put on his *Birds* DVD and David Attenborough said, "*Turdus merula* is one of the commonest British birds." I couldn't believe David Attenborough said the word turd; and on the TV. He also said, "It's only the males that are black, the females are brown." And he said, "The female is the one that builds the nest."

"That's the same as girls," Robert said. "When I get back from Afghanistan I'm gonna find a nice girl to marry and start a family."

"I'm never building a nest with a boy," I said.

"You will," he said.

"Won't."

"You'll find your wings one day." And then he looked at me really hard and said, "Till then you'll 'ave to share my nest."

"Yeah," I said and he hugged me.

"Don't get killed in Afghanistan," I said. Only I never said it out loud. I whispered it into the hood of his sweatshirt when he was hugging me.

Nan stayed for the whole of the summer after our Robert got killed in Afghanistan. I don't even know where Afghanistan is. My mate says it's where them dogs come from, the ones that look like greyhounds with long hair. I said I hope none of them get killed because of the Prime Minister. Our dog, Floss, would've been dead scared of guns. On *bomby* night Robert used to sit with her under the stairs and hold her till she stopped shaking.

Dad said he was fed up not being able to watch *his* programmes on the TV when Nan was there. "Why do we have to watch *Emmerdale Farm*?" he said.

It's called *Emmerdale*," I said. "They dropped the *Farm*."

"Oh," he said.

"Not like Corrie," I said. "That's still called *Coronation Street* it's just that everyone calls it Corrie."

"Oh," he said. Then he said, "We ought to watch educational things."

"Like David Attenborough?" I said.

But Dad said he didn't like David Attenborough so he wouldn't watch Robert's *Birds* DVD. I reckon that's not the real reason though.

But even when Nan left, Dad still watched *Emmerdale*. And he still called it *Emmerdale Farm*. And Mum still sat in the dark. She would watch home movies of me and our Robert. She cried all the time so I told her David Attenborough said we ought to use recyclable tissues. She looked at me weird.

"It's about being ecologic," I said. "We get through loads of tissues in our 'ouse."

But then I wondered: if we did, would Mum's tears come round again on the recycled tissues. So I told her I'd changed me mind.

I talked to Robert every day that first year. I told him who was in the Jungle for *I'm A Celebrity*, and I told him at least he didn't 'ave to pretend to like Nan's Christmas jumpers. And I said it was weird on his birthday without 'im there.

"Nothing's normal anymore," I said.

"Things change, Jen," Dad said. "It's what happens."

"I won't change," I said. "I'll always be a tomboy."

Then he hugged me and I thought he'd never let go.

I still bought Robert a birthday present. I bought him the latest David Attenborough book, so I could read up about the blackbirds.

David Attenborough says, "*Turdus merula* breed from March to July." But even before March I started keeping watch.

There are always blackbirds in our garden so some of them must have been *our* birds, the ones we never got to see fledge.

We all said we wouldn't go in Robert's room, not after what happened, but in the end we did. Besides, he had the best view of the garden. But the first time I just stood there by the window, waiting for the blackbirds to start building a nest, and pretending it was last spring and our Robert was still here. I started remembering things, like the way he pegged wool on the washing line and watched the birds peck at it. And sometimes the blackbirds would carry twigs bigger than them and try and get in the hedge and we used to laugh. So I pulled some wool off our Robert's Christmas jumper, the one he used to tell Nan was his favourite when really he hated it. It was just hanging there in the closet like he was still coming home. I thought it might smell of 'im but it never. Later Dad watched me peg some of the red wool on the line. I thought he was gonna kick off but he never said anything. And nor did Mum.

Then a few days after I saw the female blackbird take some of it and fly into the hedge. So I went down to see and there she was – I could see her when I bent down and looked through the hole in the privet. She was just sat there watching me back. She was there all the time after that and the male blackbird was always hanging around. Even Dad came into our Robert's room to watch and one day I came home from school and there were binoculars on the window ledge.

I should've been happy but I kept thinking about Robert; that he was missing it all. Nan's new boyfriend, who works on the till in Tesco, says if you're in heaven you get to see everything. I hope he doesn't see me on the toilet. That would be gross. But Nan says it doesn't work that way.

Mum doesn't sit in the dark anymore, even she started watching the blackbirds, especially when they hatched and the male started bringing bits of food.

Dad says he might have got it wrong about David Attenborough. But I guess he was right about one thing: things do change. Last week I wore a skirt and I've been thinking I might like to build a nest with Jason Palmer. Not yet though, I'm not even twelve.

Last night I told Robert I've decided to move into his room. I said Mum thinks it's okay, even she says we have to move on. Then I said I might have found my sensitive side because last week I cried watching a TV movie.

I told him if he sees Floss he's to give 'er a kiss for me.

And I told him the blackbirds have fledged.

It happened yesterday. Dad took photos with his new digital camera, as each one came out of the nest, even Nan was there. The baby birds flapped their wings and crept across the grass. David Attenborough says they won't be able to fly for a week though. No one said anything but I know what they were thinking, that this time last year some fella was playing a poxy trumpet. But this summer it's been different. This summer it never rained.

And this summer we were all there when the blackbirds fledged.

About this story
Winning Story in the Bath Short Story Award, 2013, first published in *Good Reads: The Bath Short Story Award, 2013*, Hearst Magazines UK, 2013.

Mirror Image

Amy Fisher folds the in-flight magazine, tucks it into the seatback, closes her eyes.

Today none of it matters.

None of it.

And she can pin down the exact moment it stopped mattering.

6.10 am Friday morning.

At 6 am Merle Fisher, *her* Merle, stood in front of the bedroom mirror in his baggy sweatpants and USC vest. He ran his fingers through his hair, grabbed the keys off the nightstand, pressed a kiss into her forehead and left.

She heard his feet on the stairs, heard the front door click shut, heard the silence of the empty house. Then she rolled over and went back to sleep.

That's where she was when it happened.

Merle ran the same route around the Hollywood Lake every day; probably passed the same dog walkers – but on Friday it was different.

Because five minutes later he was dead.

Robert Hart angles the mirror to watch the parking lot. A pregnant woman fumbles with her keys. He thinks about all the women that pass through his clinic. She walks into McDonald's clutching her purse like a woman on a mission. When Sarah was pregnant it was tuna fish and popcorn. He wants to laugh; then he wants to cry. He wonders if he'll ever see Sarah and the boys again.

A brown Chevrolet pulls into the lot. Robert sinks lower into the seat. When he looks again it's just kids, the air thudding with beat-box beats. The guy in the passenger seat rests his elbow against the open window, knuckle bling glinting. They make a circuit, brakes squealing, and they leave.

Robert redials Amy's number. Voicemail. "There's something I *really* need to tell you. About the clinic." He tries to keep his words from pitching into desperation. Then he presses his head into his hands. "What the hell did you do, Merle?"

Amy doesn't sleep. She thinks about Merle and his morning run.

Then she thinks how the world she knew is gone.

She ought to be ordering flowers, picking out a headstone, choosing a casket. But instead she's on her way to Florida to meet the *other* Mrs Fisher.

And she doesn't mean Merle's mom. God rest her soul.

Robert stares at the cell phone; imagines Amy's voice. Friday's frantic phone call, "Merle's been shot."

He remembers feeling the phone slip from his fingers. Amy sobbing. "But why, Rob? Why would someone want to kill Merle?"

Another car enters the lot. It slows down when it passes the pick-up. He's praying it's the reporter but he knows it might be *them*. He wonders if they traced his calls.

The car pulls away, turns right onto Caheunga Boulevard.

"They want to know if Merle had enemies," Amy said. "I told them he's a doctor. He helps people for God's sake!"

And that's when Robert remembered a guy who showed up at the clinic last month, hysterical, threatening to sue.

Turned out his wife and baby had just died. The name Summers sprang to mind, but he wasn't sure. They were Merle's patients. He did remember someone saying the guy had threatened to kill Merle.

People say lots of things.

"Can I get you something before we land?"

Amy looks at the air steward, her face like painted plastic.

She wonders about all the trips Merle made to the clinic in Miami; the girls who asked him the same question. She wonders what drink he asked for.

"Jack Daniels," she says.

"Coming up."

Amy never meant to say it out loud. She hates Jack Daniels.

My husband just died is what she wants to say. Shot dead. Just like that. Can you believe it? We were married thirty-one years.

The girl places the napkin on the table and sets the drink down.

Did you ever read the Anita Shreve novel? About the Pilot's wife? I guess you know a lot of pilots.

"Ice?" the girl says. She can't be sure if Merle took it with ice. She can't be sure of anything.

It's all a lie. A life built on lies. As fake as the air steward's pert breasts.

Now she realises she's smiling at her.

"Anything else?"

Maybe that's how it was for Merle. The girl asks, "Anything else?" Merle says, "Sure, how about dinner?" And she says, "Oh I'd love to Dr Fisher—"

And let's get married too, my other wife will never find out.

The girl's still looking at her.

"No."

She sips the Jack Daniels, nose screwed up at its bitterness.

Robert thinks about Sarah. She'll be on her way to her sister's or her mom's house; telling the boys it's a big adventure and the whole time she'll be wondering why he's not in work this afternoon and why Patrick Stone, Clinical Director, keeps calling the house.

"There's something going on," he told her. "Pick up the boys from school, take them someplace safe. Wait for me to call."

"What is it, Rob? Tell me."

"I can't. And see if you can find Amy."

"Is this to do with the shooting? Oh my God, they're not after you are they?"

"Don't talk to anyone. Especially not Patrick."

Seats upright, trays stowed, Amy presses her forehead to the window.

"You okay?"

She must've been crying again. She turns, studies the face of the young man next to her, the slant of his nose, the curl in his hair.

"Adam?"

"Excuse me?"

"Sorry, I was thinking about my son."

For thirty minutes Robert watches people, haunted by Amy's words, *why would someone want to kill Merle?* He'd looked for the Summers' records. When he didn't find anything he trawled through the whole damn file.

Nothing.

He should have stopped. He should never have called in a favour from Jimmy in data processing. Should never have logged into Merle's files. And he wishes to God he'd never have found *the list*.

A man steps out of a black VW on the other side of the lot. He stands with his back pressed to the driver's door, looks around.

Jennifer Summers was the last name. All high-risk pregnancies, they'd all lost babies before. And that's when he knew.

It was a drug trial.

Now the guy is walking towards the pick-up. Robert prays he's from the newspaper. He tries to convince himself it's okay when he sees he has something in his hand.

Jesus, it could be a gun.

What he knows has already got him shot at twice. He thinks if he was ever granted a wish let it be now. *Right now*. Let him be at home with Sarah and the boys. Let the past three days never have happened.

"I'm sorry, honey," he says. "I think I just fucked up."

That's when the peace is shattered.

Amy looks down at the line of red lights snaking along the interstate. She pretends it's LA, she's coming home after one of her holistic retreats. Merle is waiting at the gate with pink roses. Always pink roses.

She wonders if he brought *her* pink roses.

She thinks about the voice on the telephone; the other Mrs Fisher; the scanned copy of a marriage certificate.

"Just answer me one thing," Amy'd said. "Did you know about me?"

She'd stared at the date on the marriage certificate, counted back eleven years. She wanted to remember where she was but she couldn't.

"No," she said. "I didn't know." She added, "How could he do this to me?"

"He didn't do it to you," Amy said. "He did it to us."

It isn't a gunshot Robert hears, his blood isn't splattered on the window of his brother's pick-up. It's the theme tune of the *A Team*; the one Ben thought was funny to download and program to his home telephone number. And then he thinks shit – they haven't left yet?

As he scrambles to press the button he sees the guy walk right past the pick-up into the arms of a girl waiting two cars away. He gives her a rose. Not a gun, a rose. Hell the paranoia has finally got him. That's when he hears someone speak.

"Rob. Don't hang up. It's Patrick."

"Oh God! Where's Sarah?"

"Rob, listen to me. Sarah's not here—"

"Then who the hell let you into my house?"

"Rob, promise me you won't talk to anyone. We only just found out what Merle was doing. I swear to you. Now we need to protect them."

Robert runs through the names, the ones he wasn't supposed to find. The name of a drug he'd never heard of. Unlicensed.

"Rob?"

"Why did they shoot at me? They could've killed me.

Shit Pat, what did *I* do?"

"They needed to stop you leaving."

"I kinda gathered that."

"Stay where you are."

Who the hell is he supposed to trust? It was Patrick who found out he'd seen the file, Patrick who set security on him. Patrick who impounded his car. Jesus, he had to run half way across town and beg his brother to lend him his pick-up.

"Rob, listen to me. Stay exactly where you are, I've sent someone to get you."

"How do you know where I am?"

But Patrick has already hung up.

Amy hears the wheels scream against the tarmac.

She thinks back fifteen years. "They've asked me to set up a new clinic in Miami," Merle said.

All she could think about was Adam. That ten-year-olds weren't supposed to die.

"You can't," she said. "You're still grieving, *we're* still grieving."

The door clicked shut behind him.

She wonders if that was when she *really* lost him.

Amy walks with her head down, gripping a single item of carry-on. She slips her hand into her purse and switches on her cell. When she reaches the front of the line, she hands the taxi driver a Post-it, with a scribbled address. Her cell phone vibrates; a new voicemail. She doesn't answer. She tries to remember the last time Merle was here; wonders why she never questioned all those months apart. Was he in *her* bed when he called at bedtime? Did he tell them both the same things?

The world ended once before. Only that time it was different.

Because that time it was real.

A black Crown Vic pulls into the lot. Robert thinks about Amy; she said Merle had married a woman in Florida. But *she* was his wife! Then she begged him: "Did he know?"

The car parks up and switches off its engine.

Robert watches two men get out. They walk straight to the pick-up. The taller one presses a plastic card to the window. Robert reads the letters.

FBI.

The man signals for him to roll down the window. "Dr Hart, we need you to come with us."

As he steps out Robert says, "I didn't know. I swear to God I didn't know."

Amy hears the driver ask if she's visiting friends. She doesn't answer. A kid's bike leans against a tree. How familiar everything seems. Different city but same houses, same cars parked out front. Same people living the same lives.

She imagines as they turn corners the world is created, like a computer game. That until she sees it, it doesn't exist. Like the flaws in a *perfect* marriage.

"Maybe we need some space," Merle said. "Some time to work things out."

He said it would take six months to set up the Miami clinic. Said it was no time at all.

"Long enough to replace me," she whispers.

Amy wonders if she should have told someone but she knows they won't understand. The only person who does is

Cody Fisher and that's why she's here. How can she bury her husband when she doesn't know who he is?

Opulent houses peer from behind burnished gates, palm trees bent over in salute. It looks just like the Hollywood Hills.

The cab slows.

Amy studies the trees, the white fairy lights, the stone-chip driveway. Beyond: the whitewash walls, the slope of the terracotta roof, the pots on the Spanish terrace.

"I'm not sure if this is it, can't see the number," the driver says.

But she already knows because what she sees is her own house.

Robert sits in the back seat of the Ford, head down. He only looks up when they pull into his street. Patrick waits at the door.

As he's led inside Robert sees two more men, he presumes FBI.

"Did you talk to anyone?" Patrick says.

One of the men leans against the wall where Jamie chalked his height last summer.

"Did you tell anyone?"

"No."

Patrick gestures for Robert to sit. Patrick sits in Sarah's chair. He leans forward. "Rob, listen to me. We *never* meant for you to find out."

Robert looks along the line of books on the shelf; framed photographs on the table: their wedding, the boys' christening photos, their first days at school...

"Merle was my best man," he says. "He and Amy are Ben's godparents." He buries his head in his hands. "Jesus, Pat, how did this happen? Tell me you weren't the ones who shot him, tell me it wasn't you."

"Hell no."

"Then who? And how did you find out?"

"The Summers' baby," Patrick says. "Grew so damn big; literally ripped Jennifer Summers apart."

"But who told you, who—?"

"Jonathan Summers."

"Told you about the list?"

Patrick nods. "He killed Merle."

He wants to be angry but he doesn't feel anything. Then he senses movement, sees one of the men whisper something.

"But how do I know the clinic isn't behind this? How do I know you won't kill me next?"

"You have to trust us."

He looks back at the photographs, then at Patrick. "The way I trusted Merle?"

Amy stands there long after the cab has pulled away, even when she knows someone is standing at the door, even when she hears footsteps on gravel. She clasps her bag, holds onto the moment with both hands and very slowly turns around.

That's when she feels the sidewalk push against her knees, sees the fairy lights spin like a vortex. The world fades out.

To nothing.

"The first cloned baby to go full term was nine years ago," Patrick says. "Millie Ann Johnson. Then one baby was born each year. But the success rate was less than one percent."

Robert thinks about what he read. His discovery that *Imoxigen* is used to stop cloned embryos from spontaneously aborting in sheep. The trail of failures. Deformed foetuses, miscarriages...

"The babies?" Robert says.

"There are only two of them left."

"What happened to the others?"

"They died: genetic defects, liver problems, premature aging. It's incredible any survived."

"How much did they pay him?"

"Ten million per live birth."

"Jesus. These people were desperate."

"They lost a child, Rob. Merle offered them hope."

"Replacing deceased children! Jesus!"

"I'm not condoning it, not even for a second, but just ask yourself, Rob, what would you do?"

He pictures Jamie, four months old, suspected meningitis. The mantra of the helpless, saying *don't die, don't die, don't die*, over and over. And for the first time he thinks he understands why.

When she opens her eyes Amy thinks Merle is pushing a glass of water into her hand. He's just come back from his run, she must have fallen asleep…

"Are you sure you're okay?" The voice drifts in, then ebbs away. "Amy?"

She snaps her eyes open, stares into the face of the young woman. The true horror unravels. The blonde curls, the green eyes, the dimpled cheeks.

"He found a younger me," she says. "But I'm still here."

"So what happens now?"

"We protect the families," says Patrick. "Make sure the world never finds out what he did. Pay them back, buy their silence."

"And the last two children?"

"We watch. We wait."

"What will you tell Amy?"

"We won't. She doesn't have to know. We bury it with Merle. It's over."

But they all know it will never be over.

"Just tell me one thing," Robert says. "*How* did he do it? How did he get the DNA?"

But as his eyes look along the line of books he thinks he already knows.

Cody Fisher finishes speaking. Amy doesn't need to know how they met, how they spent their weekends. Perhaps in another life they might even have been friends.

She studies the layout of the room, the den off to the left, the kitchen at the back. She knows if she goes upstairs their bedroom will be at the front.

She realises in that moment that Cody Fisher didn't just steal her husband or her name – she stole her life.

A moment later her cell rings.

"Amy, thank God. It's Robert. Where are you?"

"You wouldn't believe me if I told you."

"Amy, you remember the baby book you bought Ben for his christening?"

"Not now, Rob, I'll call you ba—"

"I need to ask you something." As he speaks, he lays a book open on the table, looks at the outline of Ben's hands, aged one month, the cutting of his hair stuck in with tape.

Amy hears footsteps behind her. "Look, Rob, I—"

"Did you have a book for Adam? Did you ever keep a lock of his hair?"

She pictures a bicycle twisted in the road. Saying over and over that ten-year-olds aren't supposed to die; Merle saying, "But they do die, Amy."

Then she sees Merle's hands slowly unfold, rose petals scattered on a coffin. The way he turned from her and ran. And that's when she realises he never stopped.

"Amy? You still there?"

The phone falls from Amy's hand. A boy stands in the doorway.

"I'd like you to meet someone," Cody Fisher says. "This is our son… Adam."

About this story
Runner-up, Aeon Prize (Science Fiction) in 2010. I have always been fascinated by this subject matter and the very real possibility of cloning technology. We see medical advances every day and it was reported in 2018 that the first primates were successfully cloned. But just how far are scientists prepared to go? What would **you do** if the technology was available to replace someone you loved?

Chutney

I mark out time with crosses: world will end in six months and four days.

I lean elbow onto table that is stacked high with gardening magazines and press flattened tip of marker pen to today's date. Most of June and everything before is crossed out. I imagine when entire calendar is black crosses.

It is just after five. Emma will be here soon. She always come to allotment after school for cup of tea and slice of banana cake. We won't talk about date. All that matters is it's Tuesday. Tuesday is for algebra.

Except not this Tuesday.

Perhaps not any more Tuesdays.

Steam rises from plastic kettle, one with dirty smudges on side, looks like a face: two eyes, nose and wonky smile.

"How does that look anything like a face?" Emma said when I show her the first time. "You're mental you are, Georgy B."

"Mental?" I said. "I not know word."

"Yeah, mental, as a froot loop."

"Froot loop?"

She put her hands on hips and said, "Georgy it's simple, I can't see no face."

"Here," I said, running my fingers over smudge. "See, face – it look like baby."

I remember the way she looked at me then, the same way my dear Irina used to look at me when I make – what's the expression? – 'a cock up' – which was often.

"Always foot in mouth," Irina would say. She called me "glupy starik." It's Russian for silly old man. Then she laugh. Big laughs, what you call belly laughs. But right now

I don't feel so much like laughing. When I think about Irina and Emma I don't know if I should laugh or cry.

I look back at calendar. Fifty-four years is long time to be with one person. And fifty-four years is never enough time to be with one person. I pick up a tissue from table and dab my eyes. Then I think about what will happen when the world ends.
Or maybe it already has.

After I told Emma about smudges on kettle looking like face, she told me about baby. She was picking at threads on her glove, smiling. Maybe she thought telling silly old man was funny, maybe she just scared. Or maybe she had no one else to tell but silly old man. I offered her banana cake (buy one get one free at Tesco) and I watched her slurp tea, holding mug with both hands. Then she said, "I thought if you did it standing up you didn't get pregnant. That's what Darren said anyway. Fuckwit."

"You no need to swear."

"What-ever," she said.

"What you going to do?"

"Dunno. Might get it adopted."

"It?" I said. "It's not an 'it'. You can't call it 'it'."

"What-ever," she said.

Young people, they always use that expression, always say it same way like they're talking about something – what's the word? – trivial. But a baby is not trivial. So I looked right at her and I said, "Yeah, what-ever." She screwed up her face and belly-laughed.

"Georgy B you are funny. I might adopt you as my grandad."

I had to look away then.

When I turned back she got what was left of her slice of

banana cake and put the whole thing in mouth. "Got any more? It's fuc… I mean it's effing lovely, Mr Beletsky. Better than the lemon one."

Next to kettle are two mugs, one is blue and white. It's the Spurs Football Club. Irina gave it to me many many years ago.

"I know how you like Spurs," she said. "Though I not know why."

Many years before that she gave me ticket to White Hart Lane. She saved for long time; did whole lot of cleaning houses. But in the end I didn't go. I was with Irina in hospital. It was the night we lost fourth baby.

The Spurs mug belongs to Emma now. I give to her when she started coming for lessons after she told me about baby. She said she was going to get rid of it because Darren said it was best. The baby. Not Spurs mug. I try to tell her, "Who it best for?" A week later, in middle of vectors, she told me she would keep it.

"Where are your parents?" I said.

"Dead," she said. Just like that. "Dead." She said it with sweeping motion of hand like she was chasing away flies. "Same as Darren."

"Darren is dead?"

"He might as well be. The fuckwit is well and truly dumped."

I was going to tell her: no more cussing. My Irina, she was a lady. She never learned English cuss words, except for "Shit." She said it was different because all it means is *fekalii* which is Russian for poo. And every time she say word 'shit' we laughed.

"Forgot to get carrots for chutney," she'd say. "Shit."

"Council put rent up again," she'd say. "Shit."

"Tott-ing-ham Hot Spurs lose again," she'd say. "Shit."

But I never told Emma off for her cussing that day.

Maybe because there are far worse things people do than cuss.

A few days later Emma told me she grow up in a children's home. All I said was, "Shit." I never laughed.

Next to mugs is cake. Emma will be here soon. Very soon. She'll be here and she'll have something to tell me. She will tell me how her GCSE maths went and then she can show me her – I not know the English word for it – is a photograph. Is a very special photograph from hospital. Straight after her GCSE maths Emma will visit hospital. I wonder if she can see baby's face this time. Or if it look like smudge on kettle.

As I watch kettle switch off again, I think about first time I saw Emma. She was standing at edge of allotment in white shirt and very short skirt. She had purple hair. She was with boys. The one with the Arsenal T-shirt was Darren but I didn't know it then. He was the one who smoked cigarettes that he rolled himself, and spat on grass. One time, this year, when I knew who he was: the one who thought it better to get rid of babies, he made fun of Billy's runner beans and called him names like Loony Tunes Billy and Total Nut Case. So I ran out there shaking my rake and I told him: "You are one big lousy FUCK WIT." And then I said, "Who support shit football team."

Then I looked at sky and I said, "Sorry Irina."

All Billy did was gawp at me.

Clock says 5.25. Still no Emma, so I stand and look out over my patch. I hope she does well in GCSE maths. I hope nothing wrong with baby. By now it will have arms and legs and – I try not to think. Because none of it matters, what with world ending, but we carry on – we pretend – we not talk about it. I used to think world ending was a good thing. Now I think only of Emma's baby. Sometimes is best not to talk about things.

Except for carrots.

I talk to Emma about carrots.

I stare at carrot patch. "Sow in neat lines" book says. "Neat lines called drills" book says. "Lightly cover seeds with earth" book says. So today I sow. I think about last year. Bloody Carrot Fly ruin my carrots.

Billy said it happened to him once, to his runner beans.

"Runner Bean Fly?" I said.

"Halo Blight," he said.

"Hallo who?"

"Don't worry, Georgy Porgy. But it near drove me over the edge it did when I lost the lot. Not long after that I had to be sectioned."

"You had to be sex-changed?"

"You daft bugger," he said. "Sectioned, on account of the bipolar. They changed me pills. Alright now I am. But keep an eye on me, Georgy, won't you. You see me acting funny you call me quack."

"I call you quack?"

That's when he gave me card, small white one with the name Dr P Jeffers on it (nothing about ducks) and he made me pin it on wall, next to calendar, and he made me promise to phone if he acted funny. Of course since then I watch him very closely. He always act funny. But now I know I only call if he act a *different* funny.

I don't tell him I not like doctors. Or hospitals.

It was in her ovary where they find Irina's cancer.

As I look at my patch I think if cancer doesn't get me and if Halo Blight doesn't get Billy's beans and Carrot Fly doesn't get my carrots Millennium bug will get us all anyway. Billy calls it *Minellian* bug and he say will wipe us all out. Like the Carrot Fly. Dead. Just like that.

"Don't wanna bring doom and gloom," he said. "But some things are just inevitable."

"Inevitable?" I said. "Like you can't eat it?"

"Yeah that too," he said.

So there it was. We will all be dead: like carrots last year. Like our family in Russia. Like Irina. Like Emma's parents.

Then all I can think about is another baby growing – that will never be born.

I look at neat lines, the way book say to plant carrot seeds. It say to use a plank of wood to make lines straight. Last year we use ruler.

"There's one thing you must know: I hate carrots."

That's what I told Emma last year, after the frosts left and I ask her to help me. I didn't know her so well then.

I had been watching her standing by one of the empty sheds flicking cigarette ash and kissing up to boy with Arsenal top.

"Help me measure distance," I said, "between drills. Book says it should be ten to fifteen centimetres."

She shuffled a bit closer then and threw her cigarette on ground.

"But you need to find something to measure with," I told her.

She pressed her boot against the cigarette and twisted, keeping her eyes on me.

Emma doesn't smoke cigarettes now, not since I tell her she could lose baby. *Pretend like world not ending; pray for miracle.* I remember thinking same thing, a long time ago in Auschwitz.

When I asked her to measure, I thought she was going to tell me 'Bog off' but she started looking in school bag.

"I've got a ruler from Woolies," she said. "Will that do?"

"Yes Woolworths is good."

"You're not helping him are ya?" Darren said but she not answer him. Instead she looked at me. "Shatterproof?" she said.

"Good. Will do nicely."

So last year Emma measured, showing me where to put next drill. I didn't ask her this year. I decided to sow while she takes her GCSE maths and goes to hospital, to make it a big day for us both. Last year when she measured it was the first time I thought she might not be so bad. (Even if she did have purple hair and her boyfriend support shit football team.)

"Keep the ruler," Emma said afterwards when I offered her cup of tea but she said she had to get back.

"But don't you need the ruler for school?" I said.

"I hate school" she said. "Especially maths."

That's when I said, "There's one thing you should know: I hate carrots."

"Why go to all this effort when you hate carrots?"

"In life there are many things like this. You do it for end result. To make better life."

She just looked at me then like she was thinking, so I said: "Like caramelised carrot chutney."

"What?"

"I grow carrots to make caramelised carrot chutney. But I hate carrots and I hate chutney."

"Why?" Emma said, "Why the hell do you wanna make carrot chutney when you hate carrots and chutney?"

"I do this for Irina."

I remember the way Emma's eyes looked sideways and for a second she reminded me of the young frightened girl I first met in Poland.

"Who's Irina?"

"My wife."

"Oh right. Got it," she said. "Say no more." Her head tipped then towards Darren who was lighting up another cigarette. "I guess you must really love her."

"Yes."

"And she must really love caramelised carrot chutney?"

"She did."

"Oh."

"She died last year. But still I do everything only for her."

"Sorry," she said. "What was she like?"

"I only tell you if you let me help you with maths."

Her face crunched up, like Tesco carrier bag, and she looked over at Darren before she said, "You're not a perv are you?"

"People can't just be nice?" I said. Then I told her, "I used to go to evening class for hobby: City and Guilds Mathematics. I have certificate." I did not ask her what is perv, I already learned.

She thought for second; then she said. "Okay, after school." And she added, "I need cake when I study, need to keep the sugar levels high."

"Yes," I said.

In summer of last year, very hot afternoon, while we were doing trigonometry I told Emma how the chutney started, that I'd made suggestion to Irina.

"You should get hobby," I'd said.

"Caramelised carrot chutney!" is what Irina said.

"What is caramelised carrot chutney?" I'd said.

"I have no idea but I find recipe blowing along street. And it's made of carrots and carrots are good for you. So this will be my hobby."

"I thought Chutney was place in London," I told Emma and that make her laugh so it made me laugh and I wasn't sure I could remember the last time I laughed like that. And then, just like that, I was crying and Emma, not yet sixteen, she was holding silly old man. And finally she looked at me and said, "And you hate effing carrots! You silly sod!"

"Yes," I said, "I hate EFFING carrots! SILLY SOD."

Irina, she made many jars of chutney. We gave to neighbours, friends at Synagogue, sometimes people we not even know. It kept Irina busy long after we lost the fifth and sixth babies: both at same time. We stop trying after that.

Of course when I suggest Irina get hobby I thought we might do something together, like dancing, but no – I study City and Guilds Mathematics and kitchen fill up with chutney.

It was many years later, after we both had seventieth birthday, Irina said, "Tesco make shit carrots. I want to grow my own."

"Aren't you too old?" I'd said.

"Never too old, Georgy. You give up, you die." Then she looked sad and said, "You know this."

All I said was: "Yes."

There was a waiting list for allotment. By the time letter came Irina was dead from the cancer. The letter was from the council: official-looking stamp, made me nervous. I sat and looked at it for long time.

The letter said:

Dear Mr and Mrs Beletsky. We are delighted to inform you that the plot you requested at Mornington Park Allotments is now available. Blah blah blah, standard allotment size allocated 300 sq. yards (250 sq. Metres.) Blah blah blah...

Of course I didn't want it. Just like I didn't want any more chutney, or any more days wondering what a different life it would be if our babies had lived, or if Nazis had not come or if Irina had not fallen in love with me.

But then one day the chutney ran out.

And I remember what Irina said, "Never too old, Georgy. You give up, you die."

I would only grow carrots.

That's what I said. I would only grow carrots and I would only do it to make stinking caramelised carrot chutney. And only for Irina. Now it would be my hobby. We all need hobbies to forget sad things. It's what I told Irina.

It was four months later I got Number 17 bus to the Mornington Park Allotments. But I stood by gate and watched man with long hair and beard raking at mud. Then I took next bus home. I did that another three times before same man finally came over to me. "You a perv or something, mate?"

"A perv?" That was first time I hear word.

"Yeah, you got a fetish for runner beans or something?"

"Only carrots," I said. I didn't ask what fetish meant.

He laughed but it wasn't funny.

"I have plot over there," I told him.

"Harry's old plot? I wondered when someone was gonna show up." Then he held out his hand. "Billy," he said, "Runner Bean Billy." He put his big hand in mine and shook very hard. Then he said, "You staying this time?"

I looked across at the overgrown plot where Irina was supposed to grow carrots and all I said was: "Yes."

Still no Emma.

Maybe she did do badly in her GCSE maths. Or maybe they find something wrong with baby. What if there was no heart beat? I don't want to think about that so I look over to see if Billy is at his patch but he must be inside. He grows more than runner beans now. He grows onions and garlic and potatoes. Not carrots. Last month he told me he wants some of mine. In return he give me runner beans. He said he will show me how to grow swedes and turnips to make feast at Christmas.

"Yes," I said. "And Hanukah – last one."

"You're a good mate, Georgy. The best."

"I am only mate," I said.

"You're right there. Billy No Mates," he said and laughed. "You not exactly got 'em queuing up. Except for that school girl you've taken a shine to."

"Shine to?"

"You know, the girl, Emma."

"My friend."

"You help her, right? Teach her. That's what I tell people. They try to say you're a perv so I tell 'em you're a kind old man. Used to be a teacher. Right?"

"I used to make matches in factory."

"Oh. Well I told 'em you used to be a teacher. Told 'em they should mind their own bloody business anyway."

"Emma can have feast with us for Hanukah?" I said.

"Yeah, Georgy Porgy. And Eid. I forgot you're one of them."

"Them?"

"Jewish."

"Yes."

"Crimbo-Hanukah-Eid-feastmas!"

"Yes. Last time."

And that was when I told him. I told him what happened to us. I hadn't meant to. It just came out. Maybe because birds were singing and I was thinking it was last time we see spring time, all the animals putting all this effort into making babies not knowing world is ending. Or pretending, like everyone else. I didn't tell Billy everything. I left out very worst parts. I did tell him how in all of that, God sent me an angel.

He made me tea in a Liverpool FC mug (not as bad as Arsenal) and he added something special. "Vodka," he said. "Buy one get one free at Tesco. Four quid." And after we drank I lifted my sleeve and I showed him my numbers. All he said was, "You poor bugger."

He didn't say anything after that. We watched the crows in the trees for a while and then he picked up his trowel and his mug of tea and took it inside. He appeared few minutes later, came right over to me and right there in front of people getting off Number 17, he put his arms around me and hugged me. All he said was: "You poor poor bugger."

The next day I told him: "Emma said she will join us for our Crimbo-Hanukah-Eid-feastmas. Baby will be well on way to being born."

I can't look at Billy when I say that, I know what he thinks, same thing I think, that no baby will be born... we pretend, we carry on. He nodded. "Do you still eat turkey for Hanukah?"

"Only chutney" I said. "Is tradition."

He looked at me then, like he wasn't sure if it was a joke. Then he said: "Best make sure you sow them carrots next month then. Beat them bastard Carrot Flies."

I walk back to shed and click kettle on again. I look at all the crosses and think about how time can go fast and slow at the same time.

I smile when I look at photo of Irina on table by gardening magazines. Emma said she should be here, as it really her allotment. Emma said is good to remember.

"Do you remember your parents?"

"No," she said. And this time not just like that, sweeping away flies, this time she looked right at me and she said, "But you do have memories, Georgy. So why hide them away. Show the world, eh?"

The next day I went to Tesco for photo frames. I bought frame for Emma too, 99p, not buy one get one free. "For you and baby," I told her. *We must pretend...*

Maybe that is why she cried.

Then she put her hand on mine and said, "It'll be alright, trust me." I couldn't tell her why I turned away then, that what she said reminded me of something I said to Irina long time ago in Poland. And it's what Irina said to me when doctors told her 'inoperable.' I had to look up word in dictionary.

Emma helped me put photo of Irina into frame and she found right place for it. So she was looking at us when we did algebra. And as Emma sat there with her head down, trying to figure out what X equals, all I could think about was the Millennium bug and that I didn't want world to end anymore.

I hold padlock in my hand and click edges together. Billy is standing at edge of his patch. I already let two Number 17 buses go and now I think I hear another turning onto Mornington Park Avenue. But I keep on looking at Billy and now I think about the mugs in my shed with tea bags in and the uneaten banana cake. I think about how many more crosses before baby comes (if baby still coming). I think about how many crosses before the carrots are ready (if Carrot Fly doesn't get them). And I think about how many crosses before the world ends (no if). I wonder where Emma is, why she not come. I'm thinking that when I hear gate swing open at edge of allotments.

And there she is.

Emma.

She is walking towards us. She has her head down. I

raise my hand but she not see. So I just stand there, I see Billy turn his head also. Now I wait.

"Nice night," I hear Billy say.

"Yes," I say but all I can think about is Emma and how slowly she walks and maybe something bad did happen. I pray it's the GCSE maths.

"Hard to believe it's gonna end," Billy suddenly says and I turn back to him.

"The world has ended many times before," I say.

So I think about night they came to set us free from Auschwitz. And I think how endings and beginnings can feel the same.

"Alright, Billy?" I hear Emma say.

"Yeah alright, Doll," he says. "You?"

As I listen to Emma I can't help think maybe her voice sound different. I see her look over at me. I see Number 17 stop on road, hear its brakes squeak.

"Georgy B. I'm sorry."

"Is everything…"

"Everything's hunky dory."

"Hunky dory?" It must mean something bad. Hunky dory. I say it to myself in my head. Hunky dory. Hunky dory. Hunky dory.

"I knew you'd be worrying, you daft sod."

I hear Billy chuckle as he walks over and we are standing together.

"Not sure about the quadratic equations," Emma says. "How are they gonna help me in life? But I reckon I done alright." Then she goes quiet again.

I try to speak. "But what about…"

She bends her head over then and I feel an ache come to my throat. I see her hands go to belly. "You might wanna sit down for this bit," she says.

"No," I say, "I stand."

I have heard bad news many times before. I always stand. I am proud Russian man who always stands. And as I stand I hear drone of Number 17 as it pulls out from the bus stop and see its blinker flashing orange. Emma takes something out of her pocket and holds it up.

"I'm only 'aving effing twins!" she says.

Billy grabs hold of her first and hugs her but all I can do is stand still. So Emma comes to me and now she sees I'm crying but she puts her arms around me and we sway, like we're dancing and I'm sure all the people on the bus will see. Then I think, "what-ever." But then I think now that is two babies who will never be born. *Best not think... pray for miracle.* Like the one that came to the camp and set us free.

"Why you late?" I say.

"I went to look at my new flat. It's on Westman Road. The block, ya know the place for unmarried mums. Bit of a shit hole but it'll do."

"Westman Road next to Eastman Road?"

"Yeah, Westman Road next to Eastman Road."

"Westman Road on Banks Hill Estate?"

"Yes, Georgy, Westman Road on Banks Hill Estate."

"Westman Road…"

She presses her finger to my lips and says, "Yes you silly bugger, we'll practically be neighbours!"

I don't speak for a while. I watch Emma talk to Billy and I watch them go into his shed and now I think I hear whispering. I start thinking about last bus and carrots, how long they'll take to – what's the word in the book? – germinate. And I think about Millennium bug and what will happen. How will it happen? How can it happen when we have night like tonight?

I hear the shed door creak open and see Billy and Emma. Now I hear clink of mugs.

"Good job I got loads of these," Billy says and he walks towards me and offers me his red mug. "Bloody Liverpool," I mumble.

"What?" Billy says.

"Nothing."

"Stuck a little something in it," he says and winks.

We stand there and we don't speak for a while and finally Billy says, "So about this Crimbo-Hanukah-Eid-feastmas thingy, then?"

"We should have it at mine," Emma says. "I always wanted to say that. At my very own gaff. And…" She looks at me before I can ask what is gaff and says, "I've been thinking…"

So now I look at Billy, and then back at her.

"No caramelised carrot chutney eh?"

"But…"

"Well maybe just a jar, for Irina." She slurps her tea, looks right at me and says, "I thought of a better use for the carrots."

"Better than chutney?" I say.

"Yes," she says. "Better than stinking chutney. CARROT CAKE!"

"Better than Tesco banana cake?" I say.

"Yes and it don't even taste like carrots!"

"I like this," I say. "We make new tradition."

"I'll drink to that," Billy says and now we clink our mugs together.

"*Na zda-rov'-ye!*" I say. "To our health."

"And to the Carrot Fly not eating your carrots," Emma says.

"And the Blight not getting all me beans," Billy says.

"And to Millennium bug not making world end," I say.

I realise too late it 'foot in mouth' moment. It goes quiet. All we hear is London humming.

"You don't believe that do you?" Emma says.

So now I'm watching Billy.

"Do you?" she says. "You think the world's ending?"

"Well I heard it was…" Billy starts to say.

"You silly buggers!" Emma says. "That what all them black crosses are on your calendar, Georgy? You think the world's gonna end? You pair of gloomy bastards!"

"Of course not," I say looking at Billy.

"Of course not," he says looking at me.

Emma shakes her head and she must see something change in my face when I lift red Liverpool FC mug and I say: "*Na dolguyu druzhbu*! To long friendship." Then I say, "And Caramelised Carrot Chutney!"

"And Carrot Cake!" Emma says.

"And Angels when you least expect them," I say and Billy winks at me.

Now we stand very still.

We clink our mugs.

Billy and Emma laugh.

Somewhere in trees a crow cries. And on the lane I see Number 17 bus disappear as it turns the corner.

About this story
Shortlisted down to final three in UK/Canada region out of 4000 stories in The Commonwealth Short Story Prize, 2013.

This story has now been developed into a full-length novel with a working title: *Chutney for Irina.* While it explores friendship, *unlikely* friendships in many ways, it really looks at love, dealing with grief and what can happen when we embrace our differences. I also believe that in all darkness you need humour.

We Went There

We went there he said.
    Bone china tea cups, none of them matched. Yellow and white tablecloths, red sauce stains. It was raining but the chips were crispy. You must remember.
    No, Dad. I don't remember.
    How small he looks in the passenger seat. These days I can't help thinking he's been replaced by a little old person I don't recognise.

We went there he said. We sat at the table in the corner, away from the window. Mustn't sit in the window. A coffee machine made hissing sounds. One of the letters was missing.
    What was it called?
    It was on the corner.
    You don't know the name?
    There was a wireless playing. A Beatles song. The one they did with someone else, you know. They sang it together.
    I don't know.
    Billy someone.
    I don't know, Dad.

He's wearing his best suit. I said he didn't need to do that, not the black one, not the one he wore for Mum's funeral. He said he wanted to wear it, like he understands, like he knows, like he still mourns. But not just for Mum, for who he was. But does he understand what today is?
    It's for the best.
    He'll like it there.
    I reach across and fumble with the dial; there's mist on the windows.

We went there he says and now his fingertips are pressed

lightly to the glass and he's making circles. I wonder where he thinks we went. He's been saying it since I told him about Clacton-on-Sea. It's not that far I said, only a couple of hours from London; I'll still be able to come and see you. It's supposed to be a good one. I know someone who went there.

Was it Billy Preston?
Who's Billy Preston?
Who sang with the Beatles on that song?
I don't know, Dad.
You must remember. It was playing on the wireless.
Was I there?
It was the day after they landed on the moon.

I turn and look at him when he says that. He is staring out; he isn't looking at me, and I want to ask him where we went, and how does he know it was the day after they landed on the moon. But I don't say anything. I reach for the button on the radio; fill the car with the poppy up-beats of One Direction. I should've taken some of his CDs out of the box. I could pull over. He likes Sinatra. But he doesn't seem to notice there is music on at all.

We went there he says. She ate ice cream. The woman wore a pinny.

What woman?
The one who brought her the ice cream.
Who had the ice cream?
The little girl.
What little girl?
The one who had ice cream.
Why are all our conversations like this?
What kind of ice cream?
I need to break out of the loop.

The indicator blinks on and off and as I pull out into the fast lane spots of rain hit the window.

Orange.

I didn't know you could get orange ice cream.

I watch the dial on the speedometer nudge seventy-five as I pass an Eddie Stobart's lorry. Dad is looking at the driver as we speed past. He gives him a thumbs up and then giggles and tells me the driver gave him a thumbs up back and I want to, you know, hug him right there. I'm not a parent but I feel like I am.

The girl's dress he says.

What about it?

Was orange. With patterns in it. Brown swirls. She dripped ice cream on the front.

I look at him. I don't remember going to Clacton.

He's drawn a smiley face on the window, like he used to draw for me on the bathroom mirror. I want to cry. He used to write 'I love you Iris' in the mist for Mum. I think about the orange dress with the brown swirls and the ice cream dripped on the front.

Dad? Was it me?

Was what you?

The little girl who dripped ice cream on her dress?

I nudge the accelerator.

Where are we going?

Clacton.

I need the toilet.

You just went.

I need to go.

We'll stop at the next place, alright?

Where are we going?

Clacton.

Now he doesn't speak for a bit and One Direction stop singing about 'The Best Song Ever' that's really not the best song ever, and now it's the news. They're saying it's been eight years since Madeline McCann disappeared in Portugal and police are investigating a new lead. I know it's been eight years, Mum died the same week. She kept asking if they'd found her yet. Like she was hanging on until she knew they had. Like it was important to her, so I told her they had; they'd found her. Where? Not far away. Are they in trouble? Who? The people who took her? I don't know, Mum, but she's safe, that's what counts.

Yes she said.

Mum died an hour later.

Mum used to say that's why children should never leave the house; in case something bad happened. They have to leave the house I said. They have to go to school. She said even that's not safe. Men come there. What men come there? Men with guns who shoot children. I wanted to say that never happens but it does. Maybe that's why I was homeschooled until I was twelve. She always thought something bad was going to happen. I think about Madeline McCann as I overtake a fancy sports car; I'm hitting eighty-five, I ought to slow down. I flick on the wipers. I see Dad's eyes move in time to them. He watches them like there's nothing else to look at. I wonder if that's what it's like inside his head.

They're saying there's been a big accident on the A12. But it's going the other way.

We went there he says. Then he goes quiet again and I'm thinking about the rain and the accident on the A12 going the other way. Maybe we did go to Clacton. Mum wasn't always like that; she did use to leave the house. She did use to get out of bed. She never mentioned Clacton though, or holidays. They were both funny about things like that. No holidays. No photo albums. They said they didn't like photos.

I would've been three the year they landed on the moon. Maybe there *was* an orange dress.

The dress, Dad, I say. Did it have an orange bow?

What dress?

The one in the café the little girl was wearing.

Are we going there now?

We're going to Clacton.

We're not supposed to go there.

Why?

In case they come back for her.

Who?

I need the toilet.

We'll stop at the next services.

We used to live near Blackpool. I can't imagine why we'd holiday at Clacton.

The little girl didn't eat her chips.

You mean me, Dad? Was it me?

I think I remember the dress having a bow. I wish he'd use my name, know it was me.

She asked the lady in the pinny for ice cream. She said only if her mummy and daddy said it was okay. She started to cry then so I said it was okay and asked for a bowl of strawberry ice cream. That's when the little girl said she didn't like strawberry ice cream.

I don't like strawberry ice cream, Dad.

You didn't remember I didn't like strawberry ice cream?

She asked for chocolate ice cream. She spilled it down her dress.

I look at him.

I need the toilet.

Yes, Dad.
When?
Three miles.
Three miles to Clacton?
Three miles to the Little Chef.
Little Chef?
Yeah.
Like a small person who cooks?

No, Dad. I want to laugh then. For a second as I look across at him I swear I see the old dad, the funny dad; only this time he doesn't know he's made a joke. It was Dad's idea to let me go to school. Mum had to go away for a bit; the doctors said it was for the best. She was better for a while when she came home; but Dad had to count her pills, make sure she took them. One time she didn't and we found her at the park, riding the roundabout, round and round asking the children to push her faster. When Dad stopped it, helped her off she said, my life is like that. Sometimes I want the thoughts to stop.

I know he said. I know, Iris. It's alright.

I was standing there watching and the other children were watching me and I know what they were thinking. Until I went to school I thought everyone's mum was like that.

I don't like their food, Dad says and I glance back at him.
Whose food?
I'm doing ninety; the old dad would have noticed, told me to slow down. But he just stares.
Little Chef. We went there once.
Did we? I don't remember.
It was a Monday.
You remember going to Little Chef on a Monday?
No, Clacton.

I make a note to google the moon landings; find out what day it was.

I don't like the Little Chef.

We're stopping for the toilet, Dad, not to eat.

I want him to look at me, tell me he knows my name and he doesn't blame me for what I am about to do. I'll be working from home soon and they want David to relocate to the coast, near Clacton, so we'll be even closer. It's for the best.

I turn the wipers on to full speed, look at the speed dial; ninety-five. I wonder what would happen if I pushed it; how fast it would go. I remember the look on Dad's face when I passed my driving test. Mum stayed in bed. Sometimes I think she missed everything. She was in bed the day I brought David to meet them. I was seventeen, had just started working for the council. I remember them standing in the kitchen, Dad shaking David's hand. He helped us move into our first flat. You will look after her he said to David. I saw his face when he left us there. Same face when we told him a few years later we were moving to London. You could come there, Dad. Move down there.

But your mum, you know…

I knew.

In the end though they did move. David persuaded them. They were originally from down south somewhere; they didn't talk about it much. They didn't sound like they were from Blackpool; and nor do I.

I see the sign with the knife and fork. I remember when Dad said how sometimes you do things you shouldn't. What things you shouldn't? You do anything if you love them enough. What things? But all he said was, you should get married, Doris.

Who's Doris?

Huh?

You called me Doris.

I didn't.

It was the first time he called me that.

Have babies. Mum'll like that. She might even come to the wedding.

He never said what things. Mum didn't come to the wedding. We never had a baby.

The doctor said it wasn't David it was me; my eggs, not viable. We could try IVF. I won't leave you, David said when the IVF failed. Why would you even think that? We could adopt, he said. But I knew he didn't want to raise someone else's child, it's not the same.

The following week we went to the animal shelter.

I'm thinking about slowing down and pulling into the inside lane as we're near the turn-off for the Little Chef when I hear Dad and I turn to look at him. He's making soft whining sounds and his chest is rising and falling in breathy sobs. What Dad? What's the matter?

I'm sorry.

What for?

I'm trying to get into the slow lane.

Dad, what are you sorry for?

I fist my horn. Dickhead lorry drivers.

I look over– but now he has his hands in his lap and is saying oh dear, oh dear.

I manage to pull into the slow lane. As I do I see the volume of traffic heading the other way; it's slowed right down. Probably the big accident. I hope no one died.

Why are we pulling off?

For the toilet, Dad.

I don't need to go now.

It's alright, Dad. We'll sort it when we get there.

I'm sorry.

Don't cry.

I indicate and pull back into the fast lane, piss off another lorry driver. The traffic going the other way seems to be at a standstill. I'm glad I'm not going that way; although when I look at Dad now, trying to wipe pee off the front of his trousers I think maybe I should turn around. Tell David I couldn't do it. We'll look after him. I know he doesn't want that, but he's my dad.

Where are we going?

Clacton, Dad.

We were there.

Yeah I know.

The day after they landed on the moon.

Yeah you said. Some people say they didn't really go there.

Where?

To the moon.

It was in all the papers.

Yeah well I'm sure they did go there.

No I mean it was in all the papers about her.

What are you talking about now, Dad?

The little girl.

I accelerate again, it's raining harder. Dad is watching the wipers again.

I want him to remember my name. I want him to say it.

I wanted to take her back but it was too late.

Who are you talking about?

She looked so much like our little girl.

Me, Dad. That's me. She looked like me? Where was I?

Dead.

What?

The other one was dead.

What other one?

The speed dial is close to a hundred. I bet he's never been to Clacton, he's remembering something on the TV.

Dad, look at me.

He's crying again. I'm sorry he says. She looked like the other one, the one who ran into the road. I was holding on tight, but she—

Shit.

I plug the brake, shit. Shit. SHIT. The traffic up ahead has stopped. I look at the row of red lights in the mist. Instinctively my left arm goes across Dad as the brakes kick in and I try to remember what it said in the Highway Code about stopping distance in the rain. Did Dad say someone ran into the road? Another little girl?

Oh my God.

I will the car to stop.

Are we going to die right now?

Jesus.

We're thrown forwards.

We miss the car in front by a breath and I look at Dad, I can barely breathe. Even though we were jolted forward he doesn't seem to notice and he's still watching the windscreen wipers sweeping across the glass.

The traffic slowly moves forward and we start to move. I don't even know why we stopped. Jesus there was nearly another accident going this way.

Dad?

Mmm.

What little girl died?

Joanne.

No, Dad. That's me. I'm Joanne. That's me. Jo. Say it, Dad.

He actually remembered my name and I so wanted him to say it, all those times. And now he thinks I'm dead?

I move back into the slow lane; my hands are trembling and I don't know if that's from what he just said or from almost dying on the A12.
Dad.
We went there. The day after they landed on the moon. She looked so much like the other one. We didn't plan it. They weren't looking after her, weren't watching her.
What is he saying now? Dear God what the hell is he saying?
I pull onto the hard shoulder, slow down until we've stopped, the hazard lights blink on and off; I switch off the wipers.
Are we there?
Dad, look at me.
Was it me? Was I the one in the orange dress?
Are we there?
No, Dad, look at me. Please Dad. What was her name? The one in the orange dress.
Joanne.
I'm Joanne.
We used the same name. Are we in Clacton yet?
What do you mean you used the same name?
Are we there? His hands move to the door and he fumbles with the handle, but it's locked.
Dad?
He pulls at the handle again and now he's crying.
Dad?
We had to go far away.
What was her name, Dad? What was the little girl's name, the one in the orange dress?
But he doesn't need to tell me.

He has called me it enough times.

Dad, was it me in all the newspapers? As I say it I think about Madeline McCann.

His eyes move to my face and he holds my gaze for a moment, and I think he's going to say it, I think he's going to tell me and the whole time the rain goes pitter patter on the window.

Dad? What did you do?

We went there. We bought you ice cream.

He says other things, the rain keeps on pitter pattering but now all I can hear is one small word: you. He said we bought *you* ice cream.

We went there. Bone china tea cups, none of them matched. Yellow and white tablecloths, red sauce stains. It was raining but the chips were crispy. You must remember.

Yes, Dad, I think I do.

I nudge into the slow lane. I look across at the traffic going the other way only it's going nowhere. I think about David; about turning around, going back. But what if it's too late? I pump the accelerator, dart into the outside lane. I keep on accelerating until I'm hitting ninety.

Are we there?

We'll be there soon, Dad.

About this story
Placed Third in Leicester Short Story Prize, 2017, published in *Leicester Writes Anthology, Volume I*, June 2017.

I am Wolf

Nose pressed to earth
Along edges of night
A million scents
Yet only one
The smell of human

"Ja Volk." I Am Wolf.

These are the words scribbled in the pages of a journal. These are the words pressed into the cold air of a wood cabin. And these are words that were spoken by the Russian the first time she saw her. Amy Greene was there to witness it. She was there to witness a little girl in jeans and a striped sweater that didn't quite fit. She was there to witness a little girl who folded herself into the corner of a room with her hands and knees pressed to the floor. And she was there to witness a little girl who raised her head and howled her sorrow, caught in the glare of a million camera flashes.

"Ja Volk," she said.

They were the only Russian words she knew.

From a window a pool of silver moonlight bleeds out across a bed where a rucksack lays open, spilling its residue: a Coca Cola can, an empty box of panty liners and a copy of *Little Women*. On the bed is a child's toy: a stuffed animal. Amy stands in the doorway, her journal clutched to her breast. She watches shadows move in the blackness behind the glass.

"Ja Volk," she says. As she speaks a single tear rolls along her cheek. And as she turns away she whispers a name. It's the one they gave the Russian, "Volchitsa." It means Female Wolf. And somewhere in the Alaskan wilds something calls back.

* * *

Pulling out a chair, wood scraping wood, Amy sits down and runs her fingers along the edges of the journal, stuffed with newspaper clippings. She turns the pages slowly, carefully, pressing her finger along the crease. Then she reads the first headline:

> **Russian Wild Child Raised By Wolves**
> Unnamed seven-year-old 'wolf girl' discovered outside the rural village of Kostino, 250 km north of Moscow.

It was the headline Amy Greene had read that day as she sipped her Starbucks mocha. It was the headline splashed across every major newspaper that spring morning, and it was the headline that buzzed around the office of the *New York Sun*. What it meant to Amy was people had someone else's life to dissect. That was until her boss, Jonathan Pitt, had appeared in the doorway. Amy had turned away, looked at her computer screen, read more headlines.

> Family denies that Russian Wild Child is Eba Volvotino missing child abandoned by alcoholic father in 2002. The search continues.

Amy had felt Jonathan's stare stretch out across the office, thought about him in her apartment, the smell of him on her things. Then she'd squeezed the thought between her fingers until it was gone.

> Wolf Child will be moved to a Moscow centre for 're-humanisation'. Director, Vladimir Baikov, claims, "It will take some time to

> adjust. The child has to be socialised. But we are optimistic she will show significant improvement with time."

Office gossip hissed like urban snakes. Amy glanced at the group gathered at the photocopier, Claire at the centre, Claire who she thought she could trust. Then she looked back at her screen.

> Moscow psychiatrist and linguist, Boris Glebov, formerly from the Tverskaya region, unveils plan to teach the Russian girl to speak. He claims the first word they'll teach her will be 'Volk.' It means 'Wolf.'

The door to Jonathan's office was shut but Amy could still hear the whispers, could still feel Jonathan watching, his stare perched on the edge of the blinds.

On the table, clipped to the moonlight bleached pages of Amy's journal, is a photograph. It's the Russian, she's on all fours, her head tilted back, her nose lifted skyward. There's another underneath it, it shows her face, close up. In the text are a million adjectives: de-socialised, dissociated, uncivilized, uncultured, abandoned, mute, but the one that sticks is 'disconnected'. It's the word that's printed underneath the first photograph. And it's the one she remembers.

She remembers holding the picture, sitting there that day watching the office snakes and she remembers how she knew then what she had to do.

"I wanna cover the story," she'd said. "I could use a trip to Moscow. Besides you owe me."

She remembers Jonathan's face, his red cheeks, the

photograph of his wife looking at her from the desk, where piles of papers were stacked in neat rows.

"I thought we weren't gonna talk about it," he said.

"Who's talking about it?"

She watched him root around in a drawer: thinking time. Men always needed thinking time.

"You know I'm the best person for it."

He'd snapped the drawer shut and looked right at her, "Okay. The press conference is Friday. You'll need a photographer." Then he added, "I'm sending Mark Zander."

She'd stared at Jonathan, watched him shuffle papers without looking up. "You're sending Mark?"

He was the guy she'd wasted three months of her life on. He was the guy who asked too many questions. He was the guy who said he loved her when he hardly knew her.

"You're sending my ex?" she'd said.

"You want the gig or not?"

At the door he'd said something else. "You're like her, you're like that wolf girl."

"What's that supposed to mean?" she'd said.

"You figure it out."

The flicker from a gas lamp casts shadows across wooden walls as Amy thumbs through the pages of her journal. Next to her, a laptop sleeps, snapped shut. It's another vestige of who she was and not who she is. She reads on, black coffee in a mug grows cold.

Outside the wind pushes its breath to glass and rattles the door. Alaskan pines creak and somewhere an owl calls. It's a sound she knows, a sound she's learned to tell time by. She belongs to the night now. But not just any night, she belongs to this night.

She closes her eyes, imagines the blackness before it

comes, before it presses against her, before she folds herself into it. She rests her head against the pages of her open journal. She thinks about Russia, about Mark Zander. She half sleeps, half listens, but mostly she waits.

Mark acted like he'd bagged himself the best gig in town, like the trip to Moscow was winning the state lottery. He hadn't changed; he still looked at her with puppy dog eyes, same barrage of questions. Like why she moved to New York and why she twisted her hair round her finger like that. And why she wouldn't look for her mom.

She'd dumped him because he asked too many questions. It had started out okay. It always starts out okay. He seemed different but then he wanted her to meet his parents.

"A trip to Vermont," he'd said. "They're gonna love you."

"To play happy families?"

She still remembers the way he looked at her. "What is it with you?" he said. "All we want is to know you."

"No," she said. "You don't."

That's when she told him her dad dropped dead of a heart attack when she was four and her mom was an alcoholic she hadn't seen in ten years.

He'd looked at her like she was kidding. No one kids about stuff like that.

Then she told him she was screwing the boss. At the time it wasn't true.

"Sex is sex," her mom used to say. "But as for love, love messes with your head. No one wants damaged goods."

On the way to the airport Amy had picked up a book, *The Wild Wolves of Russia* that she read while Mark pretended to sleep. There was a photograph, a caption underneath it,

'*Canis Lupus*, largest wild canid'. She remembers staring into its eyes and she remembers wanting to cry but not knowing why.

"Wolves live in packs of seven to nine animals. They develop strong social bonds many of which last a lifetime." After she'd read it she'd teased her journal from the seatback, started to scribble. She wrote '*Canis Lupus* has an erratic relationship with human beings.'

Amy reads it now, the same words scribbled on the page in front of her. She stands up, carries the mug of coffee to the sink. She watches the black liquid as it drains away. Then she pours another. As she crosses the room, holding the mug with both hands, she thinks she sees them, eyes like Christmas lights watching through the trees. Then she thinks she doesn't.

The first full day in Moscow was the day of the unveiling, Amy's first encounter with Volchitsa. A ton of photographers and journalists, a little girl in a corner. The saddest cry she ever heard.

She thinks about it now. She remembers searching for the right adjective, the one with punch, the one that would make people understand. But she always came back to the same one. *Pitiful.*

She says it now. She says it out loud to the wooden walls. She draws it out, "Pit-i-ful." She says it as she looks at the clipping with the photograph Mark took that day, Volchitsa with her head raised, howling her pain. She remembers how Mark's eyes misted as he clicked away with his fancy camera. How they never spoke about it on the way back to the hotel.

That night Amy told Mark she was going out.

"Don't wait up," she'd said.

She got wasted. Some guy with a moustache and blue eyes had taught her Russian drinking games, slamming vodka shots and telling his friends he was with the "Pritty American, yes?" She told him she was there to cover the story on the wolf girl, even got out her tape recorder.

"So what do the locals think?" she'd said.

"Is fraud," he'd said. "Many stories like this. They make money."

"Cry wolf?" she'd said. He just stared at her, no understanding in his eyes. Then she left.

So there she was in a hotel room in a strange city where strange voices lifted from strange streets but everything was the same. Except for that memory of a little girl crouched in the corner of a room. Amy had pressed play on her tape recorder, "Is fraud." Rewind. "Is fraud." Rewind. Rewind. Rewind. The sound of Volchitsa's howl. Pit-i-ful.

That night she'd fallen asleep with the machine pressed to her cheek. She'd floated away on a vodka tide, pushed her tears into hotel linen.

Next day she woke up with red marks on her cheek, laptop grinning pink across the hotel room and four voice messages from Mark.

"Just making sure you made it back okay. It's 12.30."

"Still making sure. It's 1 am."

"Okay so you're either dead in a ditch or you're having way too much fun. It's 2.15 am."

And the last one, "Don't forget. We meet the girl's doctor at midday."

Health Fears for Russian Wolf Girl

After her release from hospital last week, Russian Wolf Girl, known to the world as 'Volchitsa,' has been moved to a centre for

> rehabilitation. Her doctor, Ivan Gordieva, said yesterday, "She refuses to eat, but she has to learn to trust us." Child Psychologist, specialist in abandonment, Viktor Kopul, said, "Who knows what horrors she's seen. Children like her have to learn about love. It takes a long time."

They'd spent three days in Moscow speaking with doctors, linguists, speech therapists, child psychologists and sociologists. They all smiled for the cameras. They all said the same thing. "Kids like her never turn out normal."

"I thought she was learning Russian," Amy had asked one of the translators.

"She know two words," he'd said.

She'd wanted to ask him, "You don't speak wolf then?"

On page six of her journal are the notes Amy made from *Bernstein*: *A Short History of Wolves*. She'd come across it in an American bookshop in Moscow.

"The wolf uses a range of sounds to communicate," she reads, blowing waves across the top of her coffee. "But many believe the true spirit of the wolf is in its howl. Wolves howl longest when separated from their pack."

She'd tried to imagine Volchitsa's forest, wolves with their heads lifted across a Russian moon. She'd imagined Volchitsa waiting for them to call back. It's what she used to think about when she couldn't sleep.

Amy agreed to have dinner with Mark on their last night in Moscow. She'd been a jerk. He deserved better. But there'd been another salvo of questions.

"Do you ever think about your dad?" he'd said.

"I've only got one memory of him."

And the whole time he'd watched her, Okroshka dripping from the end of his spoon. He said it was like Gazpacho but she opted for a hamburger.

"You ever thought about looking for your mom?" he'd said.

"You ever thought about shutting up with the questions?"

"People *do* care," he'd said. "But you never give them a chance."

As he spoke he raked his spoon through his Okroshka. And then he said, "What happened with Jonathan?"

"He said he wanted to leave his wife. Jerk."

"You're scared."

"What do you want, Mark? You want to bang me for old time's sake?"

"What are you so afraid of, Amy?"

He'd leaned across the table, his fingers reaching for hers. She hesitated, her hands pressed against wood. Then she pulled away.

"I'm afraid of deadlines," she said. "I need to email the story to Jonathan."

As she stood up to leave he looked right at her, "We're not all the same, Amy," he said. "Everyone deserves to be loved."

She'd thought about what he said as she worked on her report supping vodka from a bottle. She thought about her mom and she thought about Jonathan, about his wife. Mark's words in her head, "We're not all the same." Then she pushed it away, looked back at her screen. She added a quote from one of the Russian's care workers at the 'Centre,' Lolita Daletsky, "We plan to introduce Volchitsa to other children. She needs her own kind."

Then Amy had typed, "They should give her back to the wolves, then."

She deleted it.

Amy turns the pages of her journal and reads what she copied from *Bernstein*. 'Wolves form strong parental bonds.' Then she stares at a photograph of a mother playing with her wolf cub and the caption, 'Adults play for hours with their cubs. Most learning is facilitated by imitation'.

On the bedside table is a photograph of her mom and dad. It's the only one she has of the two of them together, taken in the backyard at the house in Albany. She remembers how she used to hold it in her hands, stare at it until their faces dissolved.

"I'm in the lobby," Mark said to her. "The taxi's here." Amy had woken up with piles of papers spread out on the floor, a list of titles, one called, *The Biology of Wolves* ringed in red ink.

"I'm not leaving," she'd said.

"You want me to change the flights?"

"I'm not leaving."

"What do I tell Jonathan?"

"Whatever the hell you want."

As she hung up she heard him say, "You gotta take care of yourself, Amy."

Then she'd opened the laptop and looked into the Russian's eyes. "Dis-con-nect-ed," she said.

Amy looks up from her reading, presses her feet deeper into faux fur slippers, feels the warmth against cold toes, she wonders if it's time yet. She unpacks the bag of groceries that have been sat on the table since this morning, slowly placing things in the cupboard. The man from the village drops by once a week. He has a key. Amy hardly ever sees him. He was there the day she arrived. He'd looked at her, at the pile of books on the table, a map, a chart of animal tracks. Then he'd looked at her things, old hiking boots, pink waterproof coat, binoculars.

"Research," she'd said.

"You'll need the right clothes," he'd said. "It gets cold even in the summer."

And she'd thought about being a little girl in a place where demons hid in kitchen cupboards inside glass bottles.

"Mustn't forget your coat, Amy," her mom said. Except she never did. She just wanted her to. It wasn't the same.

Amy was the kid who never ate breakfast. The kid who stuffed dirty shorts into a gym bag, because she hadn't figured out how to use the washer. And Amy was the kid who went out without a coat.

The man had told her. "You want anything special, you call me or you leave me a note, okay?"

"Sure," she'd said.

"It gets lonely up here," he'd said.

After four weeks in Moscow Amy's credit cards were maxed out, her inbox was jammed with emails from Jonathan and her cell phone was cut off.

"You think this is funny?" Jonathan had said. "Get your ass home... I thought you hated animals... Stop sending me this stuff, people have forgotten about the Russian."

"She has a name," Amy wrote back.

"I thought you flunked at science, what's with all the biology shit?"

"FU," she wrote back.

There was one from Mark Zander. All it said was, "When you coming home?"

Wolf Girl Hospitalised With Common Cold

Volchitsa the girl allegedly raised by grey wolves, was rushed to a Moscow hospital yesterday. Already malnourished, the wolf girl is said to be suffering from a common cold. A spokesman at the hospital claims, "She has no immunity to even the most common human viruses." Since her removal to a centre for rehabilitation four weeks ago, Volchitsa's health is said to have steadily declined.

It would have been easy to get lost in Russia. Would have been easy to sleep with the first guy who called her his 'Pritty American' for free vodka and rent. Would have been too easy.

It was amazing how fast everything could unravel.

Amy saw Volchitsa two more times after Mark left.

She'd stood at the back of a small pack of reporters all holding up tape recorders and pointing cameras. It had made her think about Mark, about what he was up to.

Volchitsa had looked up from a corner with bared teeth. "Wolf Caught In Headlights." It was a headline she'd never write.

"Will she ever stand?" someone had asked in a British accent. "Will she always walk like that?"

"Why doesn't she eat?"

"Does she really think she's a wolf?"

"Get her a dog."

And Amy had a thought, a moment of transient imaginings of a little girl standing upright running with a poodle at her heels.

"Will she ever behave like a human?"

Amy had turned around to see who'd spoken: an American, all wide eyes and white teeth.

"It is our hope," the doctor said, "she will learn to be human. Yes."

"But what if she doesn't want to be human?" Amy had said.

Amy sits back down at the table. Next to her journal is a copy of *Learning to be Wolf* by Adams, Brown and James. She picks it up, lifts it to her nose, sniffs. She lets it fall open in her hands and she reads the passage she's underlined.

'Socialisation begins at birth. Understanding this sophisticated and highly complex social system is the key to understanding the wolf.' Her eyes dart sideways to the photographs in the journal. One is Volchitsa, next to it is one of a female wolf, ears pressed back. Underneath it says, 'Expression of Fear.' She looks from one to the other, stares at the eyes. They look the same.

'Each wolf assumes a particular role within the pack. This role may change as the wolf matures and develops into either a strong, decisive individual or a more submissive follower.'

"Who were you, Volchitsa?" she says. "Who *could* you have been?"

Wolf Girl Continues To Worry Doctors

After recovering from a cold that had her hospitalised last month, the Wolf Child, Volchitsa from Tverskaya, continues to worry

> her doctors and carers. Dr Ivan Gordieva said yesterday, "The only thing she's responded to since she came here is wolf song played into her room. She spends most of the day pacing." Despite efforts to feed Volchitsa by a tube she is still losing weight. "We have seen her bite the tube out with her teeth," one of her carers claims. "We're trying to avoid sedation," her doctor said this morning. "But we may have no choice."

The last time Amy saw Volchitsa she had been moved back to the 'Centre,' the place government officials had gone to great lengths to point out *wasn't* an 'orphanage.' She called first, cleared it with someone who spoke broken English, almost imagined him saying, "You Pritty American, yes?"

She'd flashed her ID and a man in grey who'd looked her up and down, said something she didn't understand to his co-worker and gave her a visitor's badge. Next to them, on a table, was a Russian newspaper, the face of the American pop legend looking back at her.

He was the reason no one else was there.

Pop Icon dead at forty-five: shocked world in mourning.

Volchitsa was folded into a foetal position on a bed with a tube taped to her nose. The bed was pushed up against a white wall, curtains pulled halfway across a window made of frosted glass. The carer, a young woman in a uniform, stood in the doorway.

"Sedated?" Amy said and the carer just looked at her. "She doesn't move?"

"No close," she said. "You stay."

"What's that?" Amy had said, pointing towards Volchitsa.

The side of her face was pressed to the pillow, and in her arms she was clutching onto something. It was grey.

"Feed tube," the carer said.

"No that," she said, taking a step closer. The room smelled of soap and faeces.

"No close," the carer had said.

"I want to see," Amy said, taking another step. That's when Volchitsa opened her eyes and that was the moment the world fell away.

It was a connection. A moment when time might have stopped. Amy was close enough to see her hair. It was cut short. Her face was clean. She was staring back at Amy, she was seeing her. Amy smiled, but nothing registered. She watched her fingers dig into the grey thing, pulling it towards herself with soft jerking movements. That's when Amy realised it was a stuffed animal. It looked like a dog.

"You stand at door," the carer said.

But Amy didn't move.

She stared at Volchitsa, at the way she blinked slowly, no expression, but tears ran along the edges of her thin face. She was staring back at Amy. She kept on staring back. Then she closed her eyes and pressed her cheek into the soft fur of the stuffed dog.

That's when Amy cried.

She hooked her bag over her shoulder, where it had fallen across her arm, and turned to look at the carer. Then she walked back towards the door. She wanted to turn around, to see Volchitsa one last time, to see her holding onto the stuffed animal, seeking comfort in the artificiality of it all. Jesus she wanted to take a photo and show the world. But what she did was walk away and what she heard was the pit-i-ful whimper of a wolf cub. It was the sound that followed her into the corridor where her footsteps clanked against shiny floors, faster, louder, hands pressed to ears until she had smothered it. But it was there. It would always be there.

Amy didn't need to speak wolf to know what Volchitsa was saying.

She didn't look back. Amy didn't look at the guys who stepped aside as she marched by, dropping her visitor badge in the face of the pop legend on a crinkled newspaper. She didn't look back when she got to the door, pushing it with both hands, almost falling into fresh air. And she didn't look back when the taxi pulled away.

"She needs to go home," she'd said. "She needs to go back."

The driver had looked at her through a glass shield. "Please repeat slow," he said. "I not understand."

She'd looked away.

If she could have she would have taken her, right then she would have bundled Volchitsa into her arms and taken her with her. She would have set her free along the edge of the forest, and she would have watched her walk away, on her hands and knees, back to who she was.

Amy was still crying when the taxi pulled up at the hotel and when she threw the last of her things into a pink bag, and dumped empty vodka bottles in the wastebasket. She was crying when she called Jonathan at home. In New York it was the middle of the night.

"Who the hell is this?" his wife said.

"Put Jonathan on."

"What?" he said.

"I need your credit card details," she said. "I need to get home."

"Call the embassy."

"Please," she said. "Please, Jonathan, help me."

She remembers the silence, the way she pressed the phone to her face listening to him breathe. She remembers closing her eyes, pushing the words out, "I was scared," she told him. "I'm sorry."

"Okay," he said.

On the flight home Amy had dreamed about her dad. It was the memory of him standing outside the tent he'd built her in the backyard at the house in Albany.

"One day we'll go on safari," he'd said. "See all sorts of animals." And then he'd scooped her in his arms and said, "If you could be an animal, Amy, what would it be?"

So Amy traded one set of city lights for another. Bag over her shoulder, one in her hand and a stack of mail under her arm, she'd turned the key and stepped back into her old life.

A light blinked red on an answer machine. A message from Jonathan. "Call me when you get this." And a PS: "My wife left me." She held her finger to the button, skipped through a ton of messages, mostly the credit card company. There was one from Claire. "What's going on? Call me when you get back." And the last one was Mark. "Hey, just checking you got back okay."

She pressed delete and went to Sam's for coffee. Over the next few weeks Sam's Deli was the place Amy went to disappear. She'd pick at pretzels and white chocolate muffins, listen to songs go round on a loop. She'd make endless notes in her journal. She'd sleep late, ignore the phone, send emails to Jonathan in the hope he'd run something about the Grey Wolf. He never did.

Mark called several times, left messages, offered to take

her out for pizza but she never called back. She thought about asking him to the State Zoo. There were wolves there. She wanted to see them but it was the haunting image of a little girl, clutching onto a stuffed animal that stopped her. If she looked into their faces she was afraid she would see the same thing.

She'd read something in a brochure from the New York Society Against Captive Animals. She wrote it down. 'Displacement behaviour as a measure of anxiety.'

She looks at it now, scribbled near the back of her journal and she thinks again about the last time she saw Volchitsa. She closes her eyes.

Life went on, going to Sam's, being invisible, breathing in and out until finally everything fell apart; the way Amy always knew it would. There was a message from Jonathan on the answer machine. He'd called before, usually late at night, usually saying, "Can I come over?" usually deleted. Except for the one last week when he said, "My wife's taken me back." Then a moment of silence and, "Amy, I'm sorry too. You deserve better."

But this time all Jonathan said was, "I guess you heard about the Russian."

Amy reads the headline now.

Wolf Girl Dies in Captivity

It says everything.

They called it a virus. They mentioned malnutrition. Didn't matter. Words on a piece of paper. They all knew the truth but no one would say it.

Mark gave Amy the money for the trip. She said she needed to get away.

"You've only just come home," he'd said.

"Volchitsa died."

"Yeah, I'm sorry."

"Don't be. She's out of her misery."

"Where will you go?"

"Maybe I'll look for my mom."

And when she said it she might have believed it, for a second.

"I'll bring the money over," he'd said. "We'll go out. Think of it as a send-off."

She would have said no, mail it to me, but she figured she at least owed him that.

There wasn't much more about Volchitsa in the newspapers, just a comment on page six of the *New York Sun* the day she died. Amy looks at it now, runs her finger along it. She feels the ache in her throat.

> The Wolf Girl's doctor, Ivan Gordieva, said, "It's a terrible tragedy. We did everything we could to save her."

She shakes her head. "Not everything," she says. Another piece was printed four days later about her funeral, with a photograph, not much bigger than a postage stamp. It said they took her body back to the village of Kostino where they buried her in a patch of earth near the forest.

"Small mercies," Amy says. She says it out loud. Propped against the far wall at the end of the wood cabin is a picture, unframed, it's the one Mark sent after Volchitsa died. It's called *Eternal Souls*. Artist unknown. The painting shows a wolf paw print and a human footprint together in sand. Underneath it says, 'The Wolf guards the path walked by the dead. The Wolf and the Human whose souls have come together on earthly soils shall forever walk together.'

When Amy looks at it now she catches a tear on the edge of her finger.

Mark took Amy out for pizza the week before she left. He didn't say a whole lot, just kept watching her, like there were things he wanted to say but couldn't, half spoken sentences killed by a waitress fetching a refill or Happy Birthday sung to the kid at the next table. She'd finished her pizza, chased salad around the plate with her fork and said she didn't want dessert.

"I guess I'm not hungry," she said.

"You've lost weight," he said.

And later he walked her up to her apartment and when he handed her the envelope of cash it was like he wanted to say something then, but all he said was, "Call if you need more."

"I won't need more," she'd said.

"Okay, then call when you get back." Then he added, "I hope you find your mom."

He'd reached for her hand, held it there for a second before he let it go and turned around. "We all deserve to be loved," he said. And she'd wanted to say, "Maybe I got it wrong about you. Maybe my mom got it wrong about love." But instead she watched him walk away, the word thank you frozen on silent lips.

Amy trails a finger across the photograph clipped right at the back of her journal. It's a young male wolf. She traces the shape of his face; stares real hard into his eyes and imagines the warmth of him, the smell of him. She imagines it so hard she drowns in the ache.

"I get it now, Volchitsa," she says. "I'm sorry what they did to you."

She closes her journal and walks back to the bedroom. She brushes against the rucksack where the Coca Cola can sticks out of the top, and her copy of *Little Women*, well thumbed, spine broken. She looks at the photograph of her mom and dad on the bedside table. Then she picks up the stuffed animal from the bed and presses it to her cheek.

"I'm ready now," she says. She moves to the window, presses her face to the glass. "Ja Volk," she says.

Wolf Woman Still Missing In Alaskan Wilds

The search has been called off for Amy Greene, the 26-year-old New York reporter who went missing from near Cantwell, Alaska last month. It was local warden, Tom Greer, 43, that alerted the police when he discovered her groceries had not been touched in a week. He said yesterday, "The wilderness is no place for a city girl. They come here for the solitude but in the end it drives them crazy."

Amy Greene is believed to have been doing research for a book about Grey Wolves. "She asked me lots of questions about them," claims Tom Greer, "she wanted to know the best place to see them."

Amy Greene's good friend, Mark Zander, 27-year-old New York photographer, is still in Alaska and refuses to believe Amy could be dead. Spokesman for the Alaskan Wildlife Society said, "Without the right equipment, with winter approaching, Alaska is a dangerous place to be." Warden, Tom Greer, added, "The girl didn't even take her coat, we found it amongst her things."

"I won't give up," Mark Zander said last night. "All I want to do is find her and bring her home."

I lift my head, nose eclipsing silver
Bear my soul on an icy breath
I Am Hunter
I Am Hunted
But never Slave
For I am Wolf
And I am Free.

About this story
First published in *Gentle Footprints, A Collection of Animal Stories* published by Bridge House Publishing in aid of The Born Free Foundation, June 2010.

This is a collection I had the privilege to put together: I chose the stories and edited them and we worked alongside Virginia McKenna when the collection was launched in 2010. It was featured on *The Book Show at Hay* when Mariella Frostrup interviewed Virginia McKenna about it. The book was also featured and discussed in an interview with Virginia McKenna on ITV's *Loose Women*.

Unlike the other stories in the collection, I took the viewpoint of a human to represent the wild animal. By using the human form, I hoped it would effectively highlight the fear and pain of captivity – in a way people might relate to. Of course the story also explores identity and this idea that what we see, who we know – is who we become. I have since developed this into a novel of the same name.

Graffiti

The edges are blurred; the lines between dark and light ill-defined as if they're folded together. I watch a raindrop cross a dirty window, stare across grey rooftops, and I think how I hate Thursdays.

The world ended on a Thursday.

It's easy to stare at nothing for too long. The randomness of lists on a fridge door; baked beans crossed off, shampoo underlined, the name of a play by an unknown writer we heard on Radio 4. And a magnetic memento of a day trip to Brighton – when there were day trips to Brighton. It holds a photograph of you, aged fifteen. You can't tell. You look like any normal kid.

No one ever knows how things will turn out.

Morning news claims rising costs of living and lay-offs at factories. I picture Dad, proud in neon vest and hard hat: reminiscences of his *Health and Safety Days*: the officer, the enforcer. Life defined by punching a time-clock. But look where it got him. Or didn't get him.

"A good honest living," he said. "None of that artsy fartsy nonsense."

Of course he meant me, not you.

"You think you'll make a living ACTING?" he said; his reticence booming across a newly fitted kitchen while Mum stirred stew with a wooden spoon and looked the other way. "Look at your brother, going to the polytechnic. A vocation is what you need. People always need civil engineers."

You tried to tell him they always need actors too and what would he do without Bond; James Bond, on wet bank holiday Mondays. But all he did was laugh. You always made him laugh.

And the whole time, Mum said nothing. You said some

people keep things on the inside, because they don't know how to say them.

I can still see our house in West Hampstead where we grew up, you and I. Mum would turn in her grave if she heard me, you and me. *ME,* not I. What did she think would happen if I used the wrong word, did she think the world would end?

I picture our house, with its enduring scent of lemon polish. A brick fireplace where shiny porcelain shire horses pulled invisible carts. The Top Forty countdown on Sunday nights, all of us singing along to Brotherhood of Man and Auntie Shelly saving all her kisses for outstayed welcomes because Dad made the mistake of boasting about having a spare room. *And* a car port.

What do I have?

Cups stained with the entrails of too much tea, splashes of milk spilled from recyclable plastic that I won't recycle; toast crumbs scooped into a grey dishcloth moulded with the shape of my hand and chip fat splashes scarring the surface of a metal hob.

But it's home. And at least I didn't desert you when you needed me.

Sometimes I wonder where that place went. I imagine it's behind a closed door that one day I'll find, quite by chance. Maybe in Debenhams, a wrong door in the fitting rooms. And there you'll be; as if you've always been there, and our lives have been playing out in parallel the whole time. Mum still baking butterfly cakes that she wheels out on a Hostess trolley, Dad laughing at you doing those rancid impressions of David Bellamy while uprooting Mum's rubber plant.

I think about that as I stand at the window, counting the lives on the other side where new memories are spun. You just never realise how fragile all the threads are.

I'm still staring too long at nothing. Thinking that roof tops wear metal crowns like thorns, and further up the hill big shiny dishes. But it's all the same; people tuning into the same pulse. A place where it's hard to see the line between fiction and reality. For some it's the first thing they do in the morning, reach for a button just to hear someone speak.

London hides beneath her mantle of greyness, rain darts sideways across glass and I wait for a kettle to boil, for something to happen, for the day to end. Thursday will turn into Friday, the way a butterfly emerges from its chrysalis. And it's not just any Friday, month-end Friday where holes in walls spew out their paper. It's a miracle of urban living. Paper turned into wine.

Or worse.

As I walk from the skinny kitchen into the living room, the flat rattles, ripples dance across tea, as the 16.50 northbound train takes people into the city. I think of all the times I was one of them; neon words flashing past, urban messages without bottles.

Looking for you.

"Remember the emotion; draw upon it." It's what Robert said. Robert Frazier Pugh, Head of Performing Arts with his smile and *his way*. He said it the day I told him about you. I was a second year on an *artsy fartsy* course, living on air and dreams because someone said you didn't need anything else, while you, Dad's perfect blue-eyed boy were folded over like a comma on my bathroom floor; skinny, destitute, DESPERATE, begging me to help you feel normal.

I had no one else to turn to. How could I tell Dad the real reason you dropped out of the polytechnic had nothing to do with 'pursuing alternative career options.'

They tell me Robert Frazier Pugh bedded a lot of his students, but *I* was different. He was going to leave his wife for me, pay for you to go to The Priory. Amazing what you believe in a three star London hotel room in a champagne haze, promises forced out in breathy stutters as your head is pounded against a headboard; flesh grinding against flesh.

You always said he was no good.

In the reflection of the silent TV I see Mum's face in mine. When they first found out about you, they told friends you were sick, in a hospital *out of town*. And people would say how wonderfully they both soldiered on. But the only difference was Mum's pills came with a note from a doctor who didn't even look up when he handed it over. And Dad pissed his into a toilet pan, along with what was left of his meagre redundancy.

They would later recount their tales of woe, then too large to brush under carpets, about how they tried *so* hard to help you. But anyone can see that one chance, one cash handout for a rehab program was destined to fail.

But I don't blame them.

They did enough of that for themselves.

They say the world can change in a blink, like watching a line turn blue on a stick, two weeks after the man who was going to leave his wife for you left *you* instead. And all this at the same time YOU, my crazy brother, were leaving messages on garage doors and writing poetry about despair on derelict buildings. You told me there was no point to living at the same time I told you I carried a life inside me.

You taught me to believe in happy ever after. Something *you* never believed in.

But some outcomes are inevitable.

I reach for the plate balanced next to the tea cup. The day is edged with peanut butter, sometimes I think it's the only thing that holds the pieces together. You loved peanut butter.

17.46, the southbound train. Clinkedy clink. I stare too long at the window; net curtains drape another layer of greyness between me and the orange glow of street lamps that bleed into the drizzle.

You were the only one that knew about Robert. You were living with me at that time, promising *that this was it. You would do it this time, pay back every penny you stole.* I guess it's not a lie if you believe it when you say it.

And by then Dad had stopped talking to me too. I tried to imagine what he'd say if he knew I was scribbling lists of *'whys'* and *'why nots'* for having his illegitimate grandchild swathed in yellow plastic stamped CLINICAL WASTE.

As if all our mistakes end up in the same place.

18.10 northbound, fast train. Nystagmic eyes flick across words sprayed onto walls. Streaks of colour seen only by those that care to seek them. I remember when you tried to explain how they were the modern postcard, a place for self-expression.

"That's what the therapy was supposed to be for," I told you. But all you did was shrug.

"It's about finding a voice," you said. "An identity, like a signature that marks out territory."

I liked the primeval simplicity of what you said. And one day I came home to find you working on your identity; the initials of your name woven together, DJP (Dylan James Pinter) scribbled repeatedly on scraps of paper and magazines; the edges of the D tapered at the corner. I watched you, your jaw pushed forward the way you always did when you were deep in concentration. You wrote the same three letters over and over until they were perfect, until you had them right.

When you left they were the same letters I sought as I

turned every corner. As if London was a giant billboard, words smeared across a landscape, the voices of the unseen. And all I needed were three letters, a D tapering at the corner in fresh paint. It was the only way I knew you were still alive.

You came back to me once. Stood in the doorway, clothes sliding off what was left of you; legs twitching as if your demons had finally reached the outside. I think that's when I knew. I was looking into eyes with no reflection, searching for the face of a little boy that did David Bellamy impressions and threw his head back when he laughed. But he was behind a door somewhere, in a parallel universe.

I begged you to stay. But I always knew you wouldn't.

18.46 southbound, slow train. Clinkedy clink. I pull the curtain across, peer at the wetness on the street below. It won't be long now.

After you left, I walked the London streets, looked for you in parks and on bus shelters. When I found you I wept with relief, but then it stopped. As if the paint had run out. And now I could only see where you'd been, and not where you were.

I suppose that's when I really knew. But still I searched, rode the train to Brighton; hoping.

And then it happened. THE phone call; when a random Thursday morning stopped being random. Me, standing in a towel, still holding the telephone long after it disconnected, as if time had stopped.

For a long time, the letters that replaced yours were 'O.D.' That's what the coroner said. I imagined it with the D tapering at the corner.

19.25, all stops northbound. I stand at the window and watch two figures turn the corner. Dad looks up, lifts his hand, beside him, your nephew, football boots in a carrier bag, handsome as you were at fifteen.

I never told Dad how you talked me out of going to the clinic that day. Or that sometimes I imagine an alternative universe, one without Freddy 'Dylan' Pinter. But it's a door I'll never open.

I hear their footsteps on the stairs. Dad sits with Freddy most nights. He doesn't need to but I think it's his way of making up for something.

So I'll take the 20.01 northbound, four stops to the little theatre on Halfpenny Lane. I don't come on until the third act; it's only a small part. But it's enough. We all need to find our identity.

And on the train I look for you. 'DJP', the D tapering at the corner.

About this story
Winning story in the Chapter One Promotions International Writing Competition, 2010 and published in the winner's anthology *The Graft*. It was more recently published in *Tales from the Upper Room*, Bridge House Publishing, 2017.

The Red Queen

"It takes all the running you can do to stay in the same place."
Alice through the Looking Glass, Lewis Carol

My name reads like an obituary. Letters branded on a door: Dr M. Chase, BSc. MSc. PhD. Wildlife Protection Officer. I glance along the corridor where closed doors are edged with thin lips of light. I'm not sure how long I stand there, pressing my thoughts against the silence, as if I can hold back the day, stop it from seeping in. I draw in a deep breath; whisper a silent prayer and push the door open.

The office smells of stale coffee and sneaky cigarettes. The light is cut into strips, the blind rattling in an aircon breeze. I wait, reluctant to part with my shadow. I imagine I am twenty-nine. It's my first day and my job is to save the planet. I never cared for comic book heroes, but suddenly I wish I could spin time backwards.

I open the blind and let the light soften the edges. I stare at the green filing cabinets, the metallic sentinels that line the far wall, the legacy of my predecessor. They proffer their morning salutes but today they feel like condolences. I think about all of them. The files designated NLVs – *No Longer Viables.* I think about the ones we *almost* saved and I resign to the power of a single word.

The Aardvark, the Cheetah, the European Ground Squirrel, the Humpback Whale, the Smooth-coated Otter, the Lion, the Snow Leopard, the Panda, the Polar Bear, the Tasmanian Devil…

They all become ghosts in the end.

I stand at the window, my eyes coasting the mountain crests, tinted by the pink blush of the glass. When I look away, I see Joanna, framed in pine on the desk. The light hangs an orb over her and I blink it away. The photograph was taken in Costa Rica, on the first day of our honeymoon.

I let her name perch on my lips; linger there like the first sip of wine.

"I'm not giving up, Jo," I tell her. "You taught me that."

I switch the button on my PC; hear it click as it gathers its thoughts. I cast my eyes over the list of phone numbers: a catalogue of last chances. I lean back against the cold hardness of the day and close my eyes. The photograph of Jo with two ocelot cubs, also taken in Costa Rica, floats across the blackness like a screensaver. I imagine I'm her, pressing my face to theirs, the tickle of whiskers against my cheeks, the smell of warm fur. I imagine it so hard I clench my teeth, drowning in the ache.

When the Ocelot Project landed on my desk, it came as a blessing and a curse; a perverse twist of fate.

I hear Jo in my head: "It's not about winning or losing." I see her face, strands of hair falling out on a pillow. "It's about making every second count," she says.

I hold onto the thought, squash it into a jar and snap the lid shut. Even when I open my eyes I still see her. Now I hear Don Randolph in my head, the evolutionary biologist who has the office across the hallway. You can't save everything. I lean my head against my hands, elbows pressed into the desk. But this one's different. This one's for her.

I say it out loud like an affirmation in case the angels are listening. I figure they owe me.

I look at the first name on the list, James Liddell, a geneticist in Sydney, did all the prelim population viability studies. Someone said his father just won the lottery. I wonder what time it is in Sydney. Jo always used to say:

where there's life, there's hope. I grip onto the belief with both hands, even when it burns my fingers.

I look towards the window and watch the dust, tiny fragments of yesterday caught in the sunlight. I wonder what I would tell myself if I could go back.

"You have messages," the PC announces and I see the email from Jack reminding me that the file closes at 5 pm, as if I didn't know. In a shout it says, NO MORE DELAYS.

"Damn you," I say. "There's still one more day. Anything can happen in a day." I look at Jo's photograph until her face dissolves.

At 8.27, I dial the number for James Liddell. It goes straight to voicemail, I don't leave a message but I scribble next to his name, "try again at 9." Then I look at the meeting schedule. I move The Corvus Project to next week, resend the invite. I play the calendar like a game of Free Cell. Shuffle the cards and see how they fall.

The next name on the list is Charles Dodgson, a business tycoon from New York. Yesterday he was pictured on the cover of *Billboard*. In the article it claimed he loved wild cats. In a crazy notion, I'd added his name to the list. You can never have enough straws.

I speak to Charles Dodgson's PA; some woman called Maria Fernandez who speaks in a monotone. She says he's away until next Thursday; then suggests I drop him an email. She won't give me his cell phone number. So I find Walt McKinley's email; he works for the phone company. We've been friends since high school. He was the best man at my wedding and he is one of the few people who isn't afraid to talk about Jo, who doesn't act as if she was never here.

"I need this guy's cell phone number," I write. Then I add, "It's about Jo." I add a red exclamation mark before I press send, as if a symbol next to the words changes everything. I realise it's really a *desperation* mark. The thumbprint of the condemned.

At 10.00 am, my coffee is cold. I still don't have Charles Dodgson's cell phone number and when I tried Walt at home he didn't pick up. I call Suzanne Whitmore at the State Zoo and leave a message. She was the one who had them place collection tins and leaflets in the ocelot enclosure. Got the local kids to fundraise.

"Thanks for everything," I tell her. It sounds too much like a full stop so I add, "If you're still dating that reporter at *The New York Post*, find out if he can run the story today." I feel something tear in my heart. "Let me know," I say, my voice scrambling to find an octave above despair.

I shift my gaze to the green sentinels. Old friends who know all my secrets. Like the cigarette packet stashed for emergencies. One of the sentinels winks at me and I tip my head. "At ease, Fellas," I say. I hear Jack's voice when he told me, "No more paper, Mike. Those have to go."

"Damn you," I say and I realise I've said it out loud. "It's all that's left." I punch the words into the air.

Like John Tenniel, who came before me, I put in photographs and drawings. I include stories the children have written, ask people to write down what it feels like to look into their eyes and to touch their fur. It's not the facts; it's the details that count. The personal things. John Tenniel was a devoted ornithologist they said.

"I'm more of a dog man."

Those were the first words I ever said to Jo, of all the possible things, all the clever, witty, interesting things I could have said. I've reinvented the moment a thousand times, trying to think of something profound to say. I guess that's what we do, glorify what we want to hang on to.

It was the cafeteria at the Natural History Museum; fifteen years ago. I was bumbling around, anything not to write up my doctorate, and she was sitting at the table closest to the window. The only chair left was the one across from her. She had her head down, buried in a copy of *National Geographic* reading some article about feral cats. She didn't say anything at first, didn't even look up.

"They say cats have magical powers, you imagine when they stare at you they are brain washing you or somethin'," I said. Even at twenty-seven I was never good with girls. She kept her head down. I imagined *she* was a cat, ears thrown back as they do, fully aware but refusing me acknowledgement.

"You never know what cats are thinking. Kind of aloof, right? And you can never trust them. Evil things, whereas dogs, well you know where you are with them."

She *still* never looked up and I studied the way her hair fell across her slender shoulders. I saw she'd stopped reading and slowly she raised her head, pushed a blonde curl behind her ear and pinned me with a stare so intense I lost all feeling in my legs.

"Is that so?" she said.

I'm not sure how I responded, in *gobbledy gook* the official language of the Jabberwocky, no doubt. She continued to stare, one hand stirring the straw in her glass of strawberry milkshake, the other poised over the open page in her magazine so she wouldn't lose her place.

"You a student?" I managed to pull out of my emotional bedlam. She stopped stirring, folded her arms and leaned towards me. "I work here," she said.

"You do?"

"I'm the Feline Specialist, in charge of the Leopard Exhibit."

I can still hear the resounding crash of the clanger on the cafeteria tiles. When I looked back at her she was laughing, her head thrown right back.

I glance at the number at the bottom of my VDU, stare at it until I see it change from 11.07 to 11.08. I read a few more emails, see that the Bald Eagle Project has secured more funding, sift through another batch, see that the Brown Bear has not fared so well. When I look again I see that another thirty minutes has fallen into the void. I try Walt's cell phone and leave a message. Then I speak with Nishi, Jack's PA who reminds me we have the close-out meeting for the Ocelot Project at 3.30. I hang up on her before she finishes speaking.

"There's nothing like seeing them up close," Jo said. We were on our first date she was winding hair around her finger, her head to one side, still trying to convince me about cats. Then she showed me a photograph of an ocelot. She said her father had taken it many years ago.
"One day I'll show you," she said. "One day you'll understand."
"I do," I say. "I get it, Jo."
I say it to the silent room where only the green sentinels listen.

I work my way down the list of last chances. I leave a voice message for James Liddell. Then I watch as the number changes, as I begin the downward slide into the afternoon. I think about lunch, hear Jo tell me I need to keep my strength up. It's something I used to say to her.

The next name on the list is Kevin Bishop, a Population Geneticist from the UK. I don't even bother to check what time it is in Cambridge. I'm surprised when the guy answers after two rings.

"You're lucky to catch me," he says then he listens as I tell him how much money we need to make the project *viable*. I hear papers shuffling, then silence.

"I know someone in Glasgow," he finally says. "Bob Tweedle did a lot of chromosome mapping in the ocelot. He put in a proposal to the World Wildlife Society. I can give you his mobile number."

I feel the way hope impinges on every nerve ending. My hand is trembling as I scribble the name. "You think he can help?" I say.

"Worth a shot. I know what it's like. How everything boils down to money."

As I write the number I hear him say, "I know just how you feel."

But I know he doesn't.

I leave a message for Bob Tweedle. I tell him if he doesn't call in the next four hours it'll be *too late*. As I say it I feel something unthread and I see Jo watching me. "It's never *too late*" she says. I feel her hand pressed into mine, fingernails leaving marks in my flesh. "Don't give up," she says.

And I tell her, "I never did."

I look back at the PC and see that Walt has finally sent me an email.

"I never gave you this, okay?" it says. And he's written Charles Dodgson's cell phone number followed by the words, "Call me. We should go out for beer."

I am staring at the telephone, shuffling my thoughts into some kind of order when it rings. It's Bob Tweedle, returning my call. It sounds as though he's in a bar. I hear the clink of glasses and a sound that thuds like a pulse. I try to explain without over-sentimentalising that I am looking for funding. Then I wait. I'm beginning to think I've lost him when he shouts something about the government, followed by cuss words that he strings together poetically in a broad Scottish accent. And it seems that now he's started he can't stop.

I feel like a child waiting for my moment to jump into a turning skipping rope. I don't think it's me he's angry at, but it's hard to tell. Then he says, "It's about life, things that can't be replaced. But do they give a shit?" The word hangs between us and I realise he's waiting for me to say something.

I should be able to pull something together, something credible but the only words I find are: "Can you help me?"

He doesn't say anything at first, I wonder if he hears the despair in my voice but I figure he knows about clutching at proverbial straws.

"I spoke to WWS a few months back," he shouts. "They were interested in gene therapy. The ocelot's a good candidate."

I let the hope seep in slowly, crossing the fingers of my left hand, holding onto my breath.

"They were really keen to invest."

I concentrate hard on his words, lost in the broadness of an accent that feels like another language. *Really keen to invest* is all I hear. I glance at Jo, study the pattern made by the freckles on her nose. Then Bob Tweedle speaks again. "The cruel hand of irony played her card; they said the population's too friable. They said it wouldn't be worthwhile."

The words feel like a punch.

"Look I'm sorry," he says. "I just wanted you to know. I wish I could help."

As I replace the receiver the last thing I hear is, "Good luck."

I see the name Jack Rook in bold, subject: 3.30 meeting. When I open the email he's written, "Don't forget to bring final sign-off sheets. And I have to go over the Sea Otter figures with you on Monday. Leave a copy on Nishi's desk."

I press delete immediately. Then I lean back and watch the shapes that dance behind closed eyes. "It's okay," Jo says. I picture her face, eyes crunched into slits, body bent over.

"How can you say that?" I say. "Nothing's okay. Nothing will *ever* be okay."

At 1.45, James Liddell calls from Sydney. He says he really would love to help but his father only won a million. "Doesn't buy many yachts," he laughs and I hang up before he says anything else. I realise in Sydney, it's already tomorrow and that means time has already run out.

At 2.15, Suzanne Whitmore calls to say Paul will try to run the story but she can't make any promises. It is currently in competition with a classroom shooting that she thinks will get the slot. I thank her for trying.

"Come down to the zoo," she says. "The kids love it when you talk to them. Come and see the new Reptile House."

"Sure," I say. "Soon."

At 2.35, I wait for Charles Dodgson to answer his cell phone. I think the voicemail is about to kick in when a New York accent says. "Yes. Who is this?"

I take a moment to order my thoughts; then I tell him

how I saw his article in *Billboard* and hear that he likes wild cats. It sounds like a pick-up line; I expect the guy to hang up. When he doesn't, I figure I can't make it worse, so I tell him that some things are too precious to lose. I wait for him to speak, I can hear him breathing but he doesn't say anything.

"I'm running out of moves," I add.

"I only ever saw an ocelot in a zoo," he finally says. "They used to hunt them for fur, right? Not many left in the wild?"

"No."

"Let me think about this. Give me an hour. I'll call you back."

He hangs up before I answer and I stare at the phone as if something just died in my hand. I root for the copy of *Billboard*, look at the guy's face and for a moment I believe in miracles. I picture him calling me back. "Okay I'll help," he says. "How much do you need?" I send the thought into the universe, the way Jo used to tell me. She said it sends back what you need.

I wish that was true.

I visualise it again. That's when I realise that hope feels like remission and I press my hands on the desk to stop the world from spinning too fast.

At 3.35 I snooze the meeting reminder and stare at the file. I hear footsteps in the corridor; see shadows moving along the bottom of the door. I'm still waiting for Charles Dodgson to call me back. It's the only name I haven't crossed off the list. I even turn over the page as if I expect to see another name there, one I'd forgotten, or maybe one that appeared while I was at the coffee machine.

I look at the green sentinels and I think about John Tenniel. They say he hanged himself, left all his money to the Bird Society. It was the day after the American Robin file was stamped NLV. I think I know how he felt.

Someone knocks at the door. Certain it's Jack I hold the moment back as long as I can. But when I look up I see it's Don Randolph. He points at his watch.

"They're waiting for you," he says. He stands there for a second as if he's expecting me to do something. Then he takes a step towards me, pulling the door half way across. "You tried, Mike," he says. "You can't win them all." He must see the expression on my face because he adds, "No one blames you."

I hear Jo's voice, sweet and clear and like an angel. "Sometimes there's no one to blame." I remember when she said that. It was a warm July evening, there was a soft breeze. Our last summer. She'd placed candles in a circle on the stoop. We were lying, backs pressed to the wooden slats, our heads touching and we were watching the stars.

"I'll be that one," she said and I followed the edge of her finger. "Even when I've gone, you'll still see where I was."

"Yes," I said.

I push the boardroom door open with my foot, a plastic coffee cup balanced in one hand, a photograph in the other. Jack glances at the clock. I don't look at them as I sit down. He's already started and I see his report on the table. Three years of my life and a million years of evolution and it comes down to a lousy sheet of paper. I hear Jack's southern drawl as he resumes. I think about all the hours pored over statistics, wonder how many cups of coffee that makes. I start to count.

"You agree, Mike?"

I hear my name and I see that Jack is watching me. Next

to him is Peter Knight, the executioner. He's the guy who works for the government.

"All the population analyses show the same thing," Jack says. "Reach the same end point, right?"

I see the printouts he's holding and think about all the data crunched into a program that invents scenarios and plays the fortune teller. It reminds me of one of those magic balls.

We'd stumbled upon a toy store in New Orleans. It was the year after we met and we'd both had too many margaritas, Jo wore a plastic daisy in her hair.

"Will we live happily ever after?" she asked vigorously shaking the ball. We waited for the words to emerge. "Are you kidding?" it said and we laughed so hard I thought we would die right there.

"Mike?"

I see Don's face, his eyes widening prompting me to say something.

It's the first time I realise waiting for the magic ball feels like the day Jo peed on a plastic stick. We were at a gas station somewhere east of Nevada, melting in the desert heat, waiting for a blue line to decide what happened next.

"The endpoint," I hear Jack say, "was **GO EXTINCT** in ninety-five of the simulations."

That's when I look up. "What about the other five percent I say?" And all eyes shift in my direction. I watch Jack's expression change.

We were at the doctor's office. Jo's arm looped around mine. It was the day before our tenth wedding anniversary.

"There's only five percent chance you'll live more than two years," the doctor said.

I wondered how she kept the smile in her eyes. "It's just a number," she said. "I'm here now. That's what counts."

Caroline Powell starts her surmise on *genetic viability*. She works for the university, her jowls wobble as she moves her head.

"The initial studies looked promising," she says. "The ocelot, in spite of hunting pressure maintained reasonable genetic diversity—"

I don't like the way she uses the past tense. I look down at my hands, roll my wedding band around my finger; fumble with the edge of the photograph. I realise I've lost fifteen minutes when I see Caroline set her file face down on the table.

"Even if we could get the breeding programme established," she says. "It would mean throwing millions of dollars into a project whose outcome is uncertain."

Her last three words lodge in my head. I wonder when any outcome is certain.

"We're all dying," I hear Jo say.

Time snaps off into the silence. I notice the way the light is bending through the blinds, how the shadows are splitting the room. I'm in the dark half. I see that Don is leaning forwards in the chair, scribbling circles on a sheet of paper. He looks up when Lucy Banks, the ecologist, begins her censure. She's a mouse: her hair, her features, the sounds she makes as she moves from one carefully chosen sentence to the next. She has ketchup on her blouse.

"Not cost effective" she says. It's the only part of the sentence I hear.

I watch Peter Knight, lean back in the chair, pressing

the tips of his perfectly manicured fingernails together, like he is calculating a chess move.

When Don stands up he looks at me, before he says, "They have an ocelot at the State Zoo, a solitary female." I see the way Jack glances at Peter Knight. "I read today there's a young male in Seattle," he says. "It's common sense for someone to get them together. It's a small step, a simple one. That's what we should be doing. Not throwing money at these big fancy projects that are hit and miss. We should be throwing nature a line. Letting her do the rest."

"Sure, sure," Jack says, swatting the comment like a fly. "The science speaks for itself. The Ocelot Project, in spite of our best efforts, has reached its conclusion."

"You say it like it's inevitable," I say. "Then what the hell are we doing here?"

I see pink plumes rise on his cheeks. "You seem to forget we're working for the same team, Dr Chase."

"Bullshit." I realise I've said it aloud. "You're asking us to choose. To decide what needs money the most. Like which of your children you love the best. Choose which one to save in a fire…"

Peter Knight now leans forwards in his seat. I see Don's hands, scribbling faster. He makes furious circles on the pad in front of him, ever decreasing.

"How can we choose?" I say, my voice is shaped by desperation; I realise I've been here before.

"The Red Queen's Hypothesis," Don says lifting his head to look at me, "says everything changes in step with its environment, like running on a treadmill but not actually seeming to move. Nature finds a way to adapt if you give it a chance."

The word *chance* tugs at my hand like a fraught child. I think about Charles Dodgson. I imagine I'm on a treadmill. My legs are moving faster and faster. I see the mountains that I have gazed at for thirteen years.

But now I know I will never reach them.

"Enough of the lecture," Jack says. I follow his gaze to the clock. It's 4.45.

Peter Knight, who's said nothing so far, now stands up, his shadow falls across the table. I can't help inventing an evil laugh for him.

"Your passion is commendable, Dr Chase, Dr Randolph," he says. "But the facts remain. The file will close today at 5 pm. No more stays of execution."

I push the chair back, hearing it squeal like a cat caught in a snare. Then I hear Jack say something about the sign-off sheets, but I'm already at the door. When I look back I see that Don is holding the photograph of Jo and the two ocelot cubs that I dropped in my haste. I run into the corridor, salt coats my lips. I might not hear what Jack says, but the words rip through me anyhow.

"The ocelot is *No Longer Viable*."

It feels like Checkmate.

I stare at the telephone until it melts. I watch the minutes, 4.51, 4.52 … 4.57. I walk to the green sentinels and I brush my hand along the top. "You can't win every battle," I say. "But we put up a good fight, right?" I see Jo watching me.

The telephone rings at 4.58.

"Mike Chase? Charles Dodgson, here."

I am teetering on the edge of the cliff but now a hand is holding me there.

"I thought about what you said. I made a few calls."

I'm looking at Jo's face, squeezing everything out of the moment. I imagine myself dashing back to the boardroom, sweat on my face, hands shaking, saying, "We got it! Our last chance! Saved by the bell…"

"I'm sorry," he says.

I feel something break.

"There are just too many projects—"

I drop the telephone and I let myself fall. When I look back at the screen it's 5.01 pm.

"It's time to let go," I hear somebody say, or perhaps it's nobody. I look at the way the afternoon darkens the room. I think about the magic ball all those years ago in New Orleans; it was right about not living happily ever after. Today feels the same as the day the world stopped spinning.

It was early evening, we were at home. I opened the curtain enough for a sliver of light to find Jo. She turned her head and her lips moved but the words are gone. I drew in a deep breath and I said, "It's okay to let go."

They tell you it's the right thing to say, they just don't tell you how hard it is, how you can never really mean it.

Her hand sat in mine, moulded there like cold putty. I pressed my head to the pillow so we could lie together. I stayed there until the first star appeared along the horizon.

I lift a plastic cup to my lips and lean against the headrest, listening to the engine's drone. I've packed enough things for two weeks but I've booked a one-way ticket.

"Time is just a number," Jo says.

The camera and the scopes are in the overhead bins. By the time we land in Costa Rica, it'll be lunch time and someone would have gone to look for me. Jack will be stressing about the Sea Otter figures or Don will come in to return the photograph, the one that's in my head every time I close my eyes.

There are two manilla envelopes propped against the PC,

one is addressed to Jack Rook. It says, "Gone to see ocelots in the wild." I added, "WHILE I STILL CAN." Then I finish with, "PS: my contract of employment is NLV."

The other envelope has Don's name scribbled on the front of it. I've written, "Take care of my filing cabinets. Remember it's the personal things that matter." There's a cheque for fifty thousand dollars with a Post-it saying, "For small steps. Speak to Suzanne Whitmore; put her in touch with Seattle Zoo." Until now, I was never sure what to do with the rest of Jo's life insurance.

The last thing I've placed in the envelope is a playing card. It's the Queen of Hearts.

I unbuckle my seat belt and glance at my son. His eyes are closed and I pull the edges of the blanket across his shoulders. As I do, my hand brushes against his blonde curls and he moves in his sleep.

"It's about making every second count," I say.

About this story
First published in *In the Shadow of the Red Queen*, Bridge House Publishing, 2009. This was the second story of mine to be published. My first Master's Degree was in Ecology and this story was inspired by population simulations we ran on populations like the ocelot. It explores my very real personal fears about the plight of animals and just how much we can do to protect them. In the end it all comes down to pennies. At the time of this book going to press, endangeredearth.com claim 'there are 41,415 species on the IUCN Red List (International Union for Conservation of Nature) and 16,306 of them are endangered species threatened with extinction.' This is up from 16,118 last year. This includes both endangered animals and endangered plants. They say that in the last 500 years, human activity has forced over 800 species into extinction.

Rats in the Attic

Mum says there's rats in our attic. She said that's the sound we keep hearing.

"Sounds more like elephants," I said.

"Don't scare your sister," she said.

"Maybe the rats in Urmston wear boots," I said.

"Don't be silly, Harry," she said.

My sister has a disease. Mum said you have to get rid of rats on account of them causing disease, but rats don't cause leukaemia. I looked it up. Rats cause bubonic plague. I told Mr Fletcher that's why I had to miss footy practice. I said it was on account of the Black Death. He laughed. It wasn't supposed to be funny.

Mum says it's no one's fault Laura got sick. She said leukaemia just happens, but I think there's a reason for everything. Like why Dad cries when he thinks no one's watching. Like why they call it 'put to sleep' when it means something else. Our Labrador, Scottie, was twelve when he was put to sleep. And I think there's a reason why we've got rats in our attic.

Dad kept staring at me over the top of his newspaper, like he was looking down the end of a funnel. He does that when he's sending secret messages across the room. He thinks I might say the wrong thing, about rats being big and ugly and running up and down the walls in Laura's bedroom. But I've already decided I'm gonna tell her that by text. I'll do it tonight. When it's dark.

So when I didn't say anything, Dad shook out the newspaper and went back to slurping his tea. Mum tells him not to slurp his tea but he just says there's more important things to worry about, like Laura. And then she shuts up.

"The man's coming today," Mum said as she lifted my sister's bowl from the table, she'd hardly touched her Froot

Loops. I told her froot loops are for little kids. Mum told me to shut up. She said Laura can have whatever she wants. If she said that to me I'd ask for more than froot loops. I'd ask for an iPhone 4. My phone's not fancy like the iPhone 4.

"I saw pictures of huuuuuuge rats on a website once," I said. Dad's eyes re-appeared again along the edges of the *Daily Star.* So I said, "They were dead cute." My sister raised her head and rolled her eyes.

"I *do* know what rats are," she said. "I've got leukaemia not brain disease."

"Yeah," I said. "I know."

My sister might not have brain disease but that doesn't mean she's not thick. "Thick as Marmite," my friend, Jay, says. He means his big sister, but all big sisters are the same. Except his sister's not got leukaemia. His sister's got a boyfriend and he says that's worse.

If I show Laura the pictures of rats the size of Dr Spock (our cat) she's gonna freak. That's why I made a note to myself: ask Jay for the link to the website with the huuuuuuge rats. Jay says all the answers to all the questions anyone in the world wants to know are on the net. His dad is an 'it' man he said.

"What's an 'it' man?" I said. "Don't they kill people?"

"Don't be silly," he said. Then he said, "google it."

"Yeah," I said. But I never.

"What time's the rat man coming?" I said.

"His name's Andy," Mum said. "Don't call him the rat man."

I didn't ask what his name was. Why is it grown-ups never answer the question? So I said it again, "What time's *Andy* the rat man coming?"

"Later," she said. "Now go and clean your teeth."

"Later?" I said.

"Clean your teeth," she said.

"I don't wanna go to school," I said.

Dad shook his newspaper again. You can take pills for twitches like that. You can take pills for everything. Laura takes nine different pills.

Mum said, "You have to go to school, Harry. It's the law."

"But Laura's not going to school," I said.

"That's different," she said.

That's when Dad laid his newspaper down on the table; he did it slowly, like he was a DVD stuck on half speed. And that's when I went to clean my teeth.

I thought about the rat man a lot. Jay said rats caused the Great Fire of London but I couldn't imagine how a rat could set fire to anything. I had this thought of a rat holding one of those burning torches setting fire to all the buildings. When I told Jay he just laughed. He said rats didn't really cause the Great Fire of London. Then he said rats wouldn't be able to hold torches, or strike matches, anyway, on account of them not having opposable thumbs. I made a note to myself to google 'opposable thumbs.' But I never.

"The Great Fire of London was in 1666," Jay said. "Thirteen thousand buildings burned down. A lot of rats died."

"Yeah," I said. "I know." But I didn't.

"Three thousand people died too," Jay said.

"Yeah," I said. "That's like the number of kids that get leukaemia in Britain every year."

"Yeah," he said.

"So what will the rat man do?" I said.

"They use poison," Jay said. "The rats bleed to death."

"Oh," I said. Then we couldn't think of anything else to

say, so we went to the tuck shop for Wagon Wheels, so we didn't have to think about all the rats in my attic bleeding to death. But I did decide to put that in a text to Laura later.

When I got home from school Mum said Andy (the rat man) had already been. She said he'd put bait in the attic.

"Do rats eat fish then?" I said and she looked at me really funny.

"That's whitebait," she said. "It's not the same thing."

"Yeah," I said. "I know."

Mum's eye make-up was smudged – again.

"What colour is it then?" I said.

"What?"

"The bait?"

"Blue," she said.

"Oh."

Then I told her what Jay said, about the rats bleeding to death and she looked the other way. She seemed really sad and I thought maybe she didn't want the rats to bleed to death. So I said, "They should just put them to sleep then?"

"What?" she said.

"Nothing," I said.

I could tell she was thinking about something else.

"Laura needs a transfusion," she said. "That's when they give her someone else's blood."

"Maybe they could give her the rats' blood," I said.

"Don't be silly, Harry," she said. Then she said Laura had to stay in the hospital. She said she wasn't in the mission anymore. I didn't know she was in *the mission*. I thought that was for nuns, but I didn't say anything. "Dad's stayed with her," Mum said.

So I asked Mum if I could go up in the attic. I said I'd never seen blue bait and I wanted to know what a rat looked like when it bled to death. Mum said I was being grotesque.

I made a note to myself to google 'grotesque' later. I thought it sounded like a perfume. Then Mum said if I had reading to do for school now was a good time to do it.

Last year we read *The Pied Piper of Hamelin*. I was thinking about that too, that maybe that would be a better way to get rid of the rats, so I went upstairs. No one in our house plays the pipes or the flute, so I looked for Laura's recorder. I'm not really supposed to go into Laura's room, but people do things they're not supposed to do all the time. Dad sneaks cigarettes in the garden when Mum's out and then eats a whole packet of polos. I never tell.

Dr Spock was curled up at the end of Laura's bed and that made me think about the hospital. Laura hates the hospital; she says they give her medicine that makes her puke. She says she misses Dr Spock. Cats are supposed to get rid of rats, but since our rats wear boots and stomp around at night I think Dr Spock thinks we've got elephants. Besides Dr Spock's too lazy to kill anything.

Laura's room is Barbie Doll pink and it has purple cushions on the bed with silver sparkly bits in. And it smells like pink too. Jay says you can't smell colours but I bet rats can smell blue bait. So I started to root though Laura's things. There were tons of magazines about One Direction. She fancies Louis. She likes Harry but says she can't bring herself to fancy someone with the same name as her brother. Sisters are weird. And there was a whole heap of really crap One Direction CDs. I didn't mean to find my sister's diary. It was just there, sticking out between *Take Me Home* and *Up All Night* – the band's ugly mugs looking at me. God, she's only got One Direction CDs. Oh and a Peter André one. She fancies him too. And I didn't mean to open the letter neither but Dad says you never know what's going on in a girl's head. He says all females are a mystery. So I thought maybe I'd find the answer in Laura's diary.

Mind you, it was hard to believe you'd find the answer to anything inside something so pink and fluffy. So I made a note to myself to google it later: why girls are a mystery. But I never.

There were all these drawings of hearts. And she'd written I 'heart' Mr Fletcher. That's my P.E. teacher! That's so wrong. So I made a note to myself: **MUST** tell Jay later. Mr Fletcher looks a bit like Louis from One Direction, if you squint and look at him upside down. From a long way away.

I didn't find the answer but I did find something.

It was tucked at the back. An envelope. It had 'Mum and Dad' scribbled on the front. It wasn't sealed, so I figured that meant it was 'public property.' That's what Dad said when we got a letter for next door and he opened it. But Mum said it was rude to be nosey about other people's business. When Laura was in the hospital getting her bone marrow taken out, people always came to the house to be nosey.

"That's different," Mum said.

Everything's different when it comes to Laura. Sometimes I wish I had leukaemia. But Jay says people die of leukaemia.

I told him to shut up.

I left the letter where it was and I couldn't find Laura's recorder. So that night I listened to the rats stomping around in our attic. I wondered if they'd eaten any of the blue bait. I didn't like to think of them bleeding to death, so I went to get Dr Spock off my sister's bed so I could listen to him purring instead. It sounded like one of those rheumatic drill things and he kept dribbling on my Spiderman duvet. I didn't know what was worse. I was gonna text my sister to tell about the rats, but I never. She's not supposed to have her phone in the hospital, although I know she does. When

I woke up the next morning Dr Spock was back on my sister's bed. Everyone likes my sister best.

Next day was Saturday and when I went down for breakfast Nan was there. She said she'd come in the middle of the night. She said Mum and Dad were at the hospital. So I asked Nan if she'd heard the rats. I told her about the rat man. She pulled a funny face and said, "Can't you think about something nice, Harry?"

So I said: "Mum says when people die they go to heaven. Do you think rats go to heaven?"

She never answered. So I told her Jay thinks when you die it's just black. He says it's called the 'Black Abyss.'

"It's like being asleep," I said, "but you never get to wake up." Then I asked Nan if that's what happened to Scottie and I said I didn't like the sound of that. I said I wouldn't want to miss anything. And if Laura died she'd hate having to miss the *X Factor* final. She'd want to see who won.

Nan looked at me then. She looked like she'd been chopping onions but no one chops onions at breakfast time.

Nan said Jay was wrong. She said Grandad was in heaven.

"Yeah," I said. "I know."

"Anyway," she said. "Laura's gonna be okay."

"Yeah," I said.

Laura was still in the hospital the next Saturday. When we went to see her I put the TV on so she could see the *X Factor* semi-final but she fell asleep. Anyway, she says they'll never find another One Direction. When she woke up I told her Dr Spock was missing her and maybe the nurse would let us bring him into the hospital but Dad said pets weren't allowed. He said they cause diseases.

"So do rats," I said.

Then I told her the rats hadn't gone yet and Dad gave me a funny look and told me to shut up. "You're always talking about the rats," he said.

"Jay says it takes time for them to find the bait," I said.

Mum and Dad stayed at the hospital that night and the next night and Nan slept in our spare room. I could hear her snoring. Then on Monday morning Nan said I didn't have to go to school. She said she had something to tell me.

"Is it about the rats?" I said.

"No," she said.

"But I never heard the rats last night," I said.

"No, Harry, it's not about the rats," she said. "I need to tell you something and you need to be very brave." Then she asked me if I remembered what she'd said about heaven. And that's when she said it. She said, "Laura went to heaven last night to be with Grandad." And she cried. She pulled me towards her and she hugged me really tight.

"Will she see Scottie too?" I said.

"Maybe," she said.

"I wonder if she's seen the rats," I said.

I thought she was gonna tell me that was silly. But she never.

The next day I went back in Laura's room and I left her letter poking out between One Direction and Peter André so Mum and Dad would find it. They seemed so sad and I thought maybe it would make them feel better. I pretended I didn't know what it said. Jay's the only one I read it to:

Please don't be sad if anything happens to me.
I'm really tired now and I know if it's time to go,
that's OK. But I promise I'm still here, I won't miss
anything.

Just think of me, waiting for you.
See you soon (I hope not too soon though.)
   Love you loads, Laura x x x

    Jay says all big sisters are over-sentimental. I asked him if that means the same thing as 'mental.' He said google it. Then he said, "Yeah, it does."
    So I never googled that, I googled, "What happens after you die?"
    There was loads more stuff about heaven than the 'Black Abyss' so I told Jay he was wrong about that. I told him there was heaven and God was the dude in charge.
    "Yeah," he said. "I know." But he didn't.

Sometimes at night I still think about the rats that used to be in our attic. And sometimes I text my sister.
    I told her who won the *X Factor*, in case heaven hasn't gone digital yet, and I told her we played One Direction at her funeral. She'd've liked that. We played 'What Makes You Beautiful' – it's her favourite. Mum cried and she says she can't listen to it now. "She was beautiful, wasn't she?" she said.
    "Yeah." I never told anyone though, I mean she's me sister, how could I tell her that? Although I did whisper it when I said goodbye at the crematorium and the coffin was disappearing. I said it into my sleeve as I wiped snot off and pretended I wasn't crying. Mum says she meant to write to One Direction to tell them about Laura. But it's too late now. That's what she says. "It's too late." Like we've no reason to live anymore – but there is. There always is. Jay says it.
    And I told her say hi to Grandad from Nan. And I told her to give Scottie a kiss for me. "Beam me up," I said. I know it would've made her laugh. I asked her if you can get Froot Loops in heaven.

She hasn't replied yet.

Last night I told her Dr Spock sleeps on *my* bed now. Then I put a PS: well he does *sometimes*. I said I think he still likes her best.

I suppose Dr Spock will be with her in heaven one day. I suppose we all will.

Tonight I sent her a text that said: I hope the rats are running up and down the walls in heaven. And PS, Jay says the rats in heaven are BIGGER than elephants.

She's gonna freak.

I haven't decided what to tell her tomorrow. But I have written to Louis from One Direction and told him all about her.

She'll like that.

About this story
Winning story of the Sunpenny Press Short Story Competition 2010, later shortlisted and recorded for radio in the Carried in Waves Writing Competition, 2015.

Thinking in Circles

In order to understand something, we must exist outside it.

We are all made of numbers.
  Aged 13, Size 8 shoes, Form 5, the 14.35.
  We are all on a journey to somewhere from somewhere else with our eyes half-closed.
  And sometimes we get stuck.

You are standing there. Head tucked down; reminds me of a penguin. The strap of your big blue school bag cuts across your blazer and it's as if there's a thread attaching your head to your shoes. Not shiny new shoes. These are scuffed, end of term Clark's one size too small shoes; they didn't buy new shoes. Because of what happened over the summer.
  It's the thing – the thing no one will want to talk about – but they will talk about it. They'll whisper. They'll pretend they're not talking about it.
  People say bad news is always better when it happens to somebody else but even when it happens to somebody else; sometimes it's happening to you.

You shuffle last year's shoes to the front; to the desk you used last year. And the year before. And the year before that. Soon they'll all come in and sit where they always sit and nobody will ask. But they'll all know.
  They'll all know because it was in the *Echo*. It was in the *Echo* over the summer. Shock had filled up the kitchen: a line of uttered Oh Gods.
  In the sound you were sure you heard something break. Not like a snap. Not like an ornament shattering

into a million pieces. Not like that. And not like the jolt of something stopping suddenly because that happens all at once. This was like a slow unpicking along the seams.

It happened because of what happened over the summer. It happened to your dad when he went quietly mad – and your nan had to move in.

It was in the *Echo*. Everyone knows. About the thing – not your dad going quietly mad, or your nan moving in. About the thing. The thing that happened over the summer.

The train left London at 14.35. The name on the front said Southend Victoria.

Don't go near the railway lines everyone says. It's dangerous. There should be fences. Nans and grandads, dads and mums say it: don't go near the railway lines. And teachers say it. I said it.

But they do go near the tracks.

You speak to your mum every day.

You spoke to her that day, in the kitchen. Your dad was speaking to the vicar in the dining room. Even though people say you can't, you know that when someone's gone you can still speak to them – but you can't touch. You can't touch ghosts.

There's a map. It's on the wall in your dad's office – an obsession with train routes, like your own version of join the dots. One day we'll ride them all he said. Britain, Europe, even America. We'll ride them all. Yeah– we'll ride them all, Dad. It's how you imagined life's big adventure. You start somewhere and you end somewhere else but it's not where you end up, it's how you got there.

Now all that's left are pieces; spattered along the tracks.

And your dad says he will never ride the trains again.

That sound. That's what makes me look up. The familiar sound of a blue school bag thudding to the floor in a silent classroom; the sound of a zipper on a school bag unzipping like another seam unpicking. You lean down, lift out a pencil case and an exercise book. You set them down on the desk.

You used to play hide and seek, with your sister, but after it happened you'd find her in the wardrobe – sobbing. She was so easy to find. She tells you she is too old for silly games. Leave me alone, Stephen she says. Stop finding me.

But you promised to always protect her.

It wasn't her fault your mum was the way she was.

It wasn't her fault what happened in the summer.

It's like your mum got stuck. Like she was always stuck. She used to stash pills in the drawer… in case. She never said in case of what.

They think I'm like her, your sister said.

You're not, Susie. You're not.

I hear voices.

What kind of voices?

Mum heard voices, she said.

And you said, yeah I know.

First stop Stratford. 14.43. Mum switches off the news. She thinks about leaving a note but there isn't time; the front door slams shut behind her. An ornament rattles and falls from a shelf but she doesn't see the pieces shatter.

Susie said it hurts and you can't make it stop but before you could tell her it was okay, she really wasn't like your mum and she could speak to someone, the school could help, she said – anyway, what are you doing here, Stephen?

Someone has to be here, you said.

Your dad wasn't; well he was – but it was like he wasn't. And Nan just kept making tea and crying a lot.

I miss her, Susie said, I miss Mum.

The sound of a bell; the clatter of footsteps, the classroom door opening and shutting, pockets of sound: shouting, laughing, screaming. The outside comes in.

Arrives Shenfield 14.49. Mum pulls the edges of her knitted brown cardigan closer, walks faster, doesn't look back, walks to the end of the lane and turns the corner.

The pieces of the ornament are scattered across the kitchen tiles.

You don't look up. I watch you pick at a thread of black wool from the homemade jumper your nan knitted, as the rest of the children file in, in their new shiny shoes.

The room hushes, words are swept into corners.

Eyes fixed on the place where you sit at the front. I think I ought to say something but I don't.

She had a timetable. It was for all the trains from London to Southend Victoria and back again. She kept it in the kitchen drawer. She used to argue with your dad, all the time, every day. One day I'm going to jump she said. You weren't supposed to hear.

Voices lift from quiet to chitter chatter in the classroom. I watch you sit with your head down and I see you roll a pencil between your fingers. No one sits next to you. No one ever has.

Formalities: handouts, notices, anti-bullying policies.

There's been a crackdown. They talk about it in the staffroom.

I miss Mum too. It's what you tell your sister. You are not like her, Susie.

Next stop Billericay 15.05. Mum is nearly there. Like she is drawn there by a spell. Don't stop. Keep running along the path until you get there.

When she picked you up from school you would know if she had been watching trains again, but not the way your dad did. He would say she needed to see the doctor again. She needed to be sent away again.

Don't jump.

You shove your pencil case and notebook into the big blue school bag. The bell has gone for the end of registration and you haven't said a word.

Train reaches Wickford: 15.11.

Eight minutes left.

How many times does a heart beat in eight minutes? How many heart beats are left?

Don't jump.

But you can't change it.

The timetable was missing from the kitchen drawer: trains from London to Southend Victoria and back. A scream died where it formed. Dear God. She didn't see the ornament rattle and fall, she didn't see the Virgin Mary shatter into a million pieces on the kitchen floor. All she did was run.

But it was too late; you can't change it.

I follow you out of the classroom.

I feel like I'm back where it started.

Train arrives at Rayleigh. It's 15.17. A minute late. Two minutes before it happens. Mum runs, looks at her watch and keeps on running.

She knew all the times; she knew when they were running late. Like a minute might make the difference: how many more times does the heart beat in that minute? She would've told herself there was still time. That minute will make all the difference.

But she was wrong.

Train leaves Rayleigh at 15.18.

She looks at her watch again. 15.19.

Time stops dead – on the tracks.

All at once.

It stops.

And that's when I know who you are; the little boy standing in the playground. I know. I've stood here before, over and over on the same day, in the same moment – but I've never seen your face. Until now. I've never stood on the outside looking in.

Mum was there. She saw me jump. She sensed something bad was going to happen that day. She knew. The timetable was gone. There was a letter on the kitchen table to go to the school to talk about the bullying. She swears she didn't know it was happening.

I hear her voice now. She'll be in the kitchen. The clock goes tick tock tick tock tick tock. The nurses say she will be well enough to go home soon. Dad will be okay. It just takes time. Nan will stay as long as she needs to and as long as my sister needs her. They visit Mum every day in that place. Nan tells her over and over she is not like her mum.

Dad had a breakdown they said – grief does that – but not like the way a train breaks down; this is different. But not so bad he had to go to that place too.

Her screams were drowned out by the sound of the train's brakes squealing.

My brains were smeared like jelly along the track.

It was in the *Echo* the next day.

We reach the other side of the playground and you look up. I look down at my Size 8 shoes; they are still scuffed. Our shoes.

We have lived this day so many times; like we can't move past it.

But now I know who you are, who we are – and we can. We must move past it.

The signal must change to green.

Mum must stop blaming herself.

Dad needs to ride the trains, Britain, Europe, even America, as soon as he gets better.

My sister needs to know she isn't like her. It was me who was like her.

I reach out to touch you, me, us, a little boy in a playground, who isn't really there, my sister won't hear the voices anymore… she will be okay now… she won't be bullied the way I was. I know it won't be easy. They all have a long journey ahead of them… but they will be okay now… because… finally…

I've gone.

In order to understand something, we must exist outside it.

We are all made of numbers.

Aged 13, Size 8 shoes, Form 5, 8.23 am, the 14.35.

We are all on a journey to somewhere from somewhere else with our eyes half-closed.

But I'm not stuck anymore.

About this story
Runner-up in the Book A Break Short Story Competition, 2017, first published in *With Our Eyes Open* Anthology, June 2017. The theme of the competition was *journeys*.

Director's Cut

Arnold Pepper makes his way slowly across the lot; he wears a suit, a black trilby perched on his balding head. As he walks he taps out time with a hickory walking cane. When he gets to the corner he stops and feels for the edges of a sealed manilla envelope that he has placed in his breast pocket. It beats like a second pulse. He checks the time on a watch that stopped fifty years ago, runs his fingers along the inscription and thinks about endings.

Nothing lasts forever, Arnie he hears in his head. He teases a tissue from his pocket and catches the memory.

Connie holding his hand.

Connie looking into his eyes.

Connie walking away.

He drags his thoughts back to now. And the fate of Christian Black. His greatest creation: the revered hero of Millennium Pictures.

One question buzzes on people's lips, weaves through speculating minds and folds itself into the LA smog: will they do it? Will they kill Christian Black? And the answer to that is in Arnold Pepper's pocket.

Arnold looks at the line of perfect trees planted in a world of rubber bricks and hollow facades. And he realises that everything that happened, happened right here. Moments captured in frames, each one playing out in his head, the counter starts at 00:00:00:00. He sees it at the corner of everything.

The Arnold Pepper story: a cast of writers, producers, editors, key grips, costume designers, set painters. Even *stars* before they twinkled. Now most are nameless faces. But not Jimmy Cox. The man with the big dreams. Two rookies, two stories, two endings. He thinks about what happened and closes his eyes.

When he opens them again the light has changed. Aerial shot. Arnold looks at the sun, climbing a cerulean backdrop. When he looks back he sees shapes. They float like ghosts in front of him and paint scars on white walls. Hard to capture.

Now he's aware of people around him; sound bites snapping off. A girl laughing, someone yelling, maybe even a dog barking. He tightens his grip on his cane and remembers his appointment with destiny: the fate of Christian Black.

Christian Black is the man that lived the life he never did. A life that unfolded in storyboards. Words squeezed out of actors, like puppets. One common purpose: to tell the story the audience want to hear. Love, hope, passion, drama. All the gloss with none of the in between.

He wonders if he could, would he go back and rework his own life the same way. But there are some scripts no one wants to read.

"Hey, Mr P, how ya doin', Sir?"

When he turns he sees Jazz, the guy that fetches the mail. Lips glossed into a Marilyn Monroe pout as if he's kissing air.

"The end of an era," Jazz says. "So how's it feel?"

Arnold leans both hands on his cane and looks right at him. "You know I started in the mail room," he says, "did I tell you that, Kid?" He squints, studying the features of Jazz's face. He wonders how he gets his bleached hair to stand up like quills.

"I think you might have told me," Jazz says grinning. "The mail boy in like 1857 or somethin' right?"

Arnold doesn't laugh. Instead he looks at the AIDS pin Jazz wears on his T-shirt like a statement. He wants to ask him about *his friend.* If he's out of the hospital. But he says nothing. Deletes the scene.

"And I suppose you're gonna remind me how you knew them all?" Jazz says. "Like Bernard G, THE director of all time." He smiles in wide angle. "Apart from you, of course, Mr P."

A group of young actors rush past. They're talking about *his* movie. About Christian Black. *Every girl's lover. Every guy's best friend.*

"They filmed two endings," the girl says.

"Hey, you bored with the mail guy now?" Jazz says.

When he looks back Jazz is standing with his hands rested on his hips. "A lot of memories, huh?"

Too many memories, folded into rolls of film. Curled like sleeping cats.

The job was a favour for his uncle, who was doing a favour for his mother.

"That boy will daydream his life away," she said. "He needs direction, a focus."

Good choice of words.

Now the counter reads sixty years and twenty-six semi-decent movies. So much for wagers. But everything has an ending.

When he looks back he sees that Jazz is still watching him.

"No anecdotes about the GREAT Bernard Golden today?" he says, hints of a Puerto Rican accent. "How you didn't even know who he was?"

```
FLASHBACK TO: MAY 1951

EXT. FILM STUDIOS - MORNING

SEVENTEEN-YEAR-OLD GEEK MAIL BOY gets
lost on his first day at Millennium
Pictures.
```

BERNARD GOLDEN - handsome dark looks,
grey suit, cigarette propped between his
lips - watches the MAIL BOY crossing the
lot.

BERNARD G: Hey Kid. Come 'ere. Don't you
know this is a restricted area?

ARNOLD PEPPER - THE MAIL BOY: (*looking
around nervously*) No Sir. I was just
looking for Bernard Golden.

BERNARD G: (*smirking*) You mean that know
it all, arrogant A-hole? You better watch
him, Kiddo. He bites.

Arnold looks across the office block, blinds at the windows. Thinks about all those that have gone before him. But there are some endings that can't be scripted. He thinks about a car taking a bend too fast. About Connie and Jimmy.

"There's a hundred ways to tell a story, Kiddo," Bernie G told him. "But what they'll remember is how it ended."

Arnold turns the phrase over in his head, inadvertently taps the envelope that sits next to his heart.

"It's what lives in their heads when the ice cream's melted and the popcorn's rotted."

"Hey Arnie, where are you? You thinking about the good ol' days?" Jazz's voice drifts in. "You lived the American dream, Man."

The phrase jars, like film despooling.

"The thing about dreams," he hears Bernie G say. "Is if you hold 'em in your hands too long, they burn."

FLASHBACK TO: JANUARY 1952
INT. STUDIO CAFETERA, LUNCH TIME

EIGHTEEN-YEAR-OLD ARNOLD PEPPER is in the lunch line. He stands with hands in pockets.

JIMMY COX (PROPS BOY, handsome) joins him, throws a cigarette and catches it between his lips, practises his best movie smoulder.

JIMMY: Pretty good, huh? Step aside for the next Hollywood Star.

ARNOLD: Yeah right.

JIMMY: A guy's gotta have a dream, Arn. What's yours?

ARNOLD: I'm the mail boy.

JIMMY: But no one comes to Hollywood without a dream.

ARNOLD: (*smirking*) Is that so? Well not me.

JIMMY: That's bullshit. I see the way you suck up to Bernie G. Everyone has a dream.

ARNOLD: (*sarcastic*) Okay kidding. One day EVERYONE will know my films.

JIMMY: There you go, I knew it!

DISSOLVES OUT

Tell them what they want to hear Bernie G said.
But Arnold never imagined, not even for a second, that it would happen.

"The life of Arnold Pepper – Movie Director": a title on a spec script destined for the slush pile. He hears the voiceover for a trailer no one will make, "This is a classic tale of *happenchance*... the ultimate Hollywood FLUKE…"

Forty years later when Christian Black first walked out of that fire with a five-year-old girl in his arms, the instant hero, Arnold Pepper scooped the first three-movie-deal of his career. He hears Bernie G's words when he won an Academy Award in 1954 for *Burning Desire*, "Everyone loves a fireman, Kiddo."
"Hey Mr P, catch you later, okay Man?"
Jazz is squinting at him, earring shimmering, glare spoils the shot.
"Sure, you take care," Arnold says. "See ya, Kid."
He watches him walk away. The swinging hips have to go. Spoils the final scene.
Arnold steps off the sidewalk, waits for a buggy to pass. That's when he sees her. The girl. Soft lighting. She walks across the lot, auburn curls bouncing as she moves.
Freeze frame.

```
FLASHBACK TO: JULY 1955

INT: STUDIO CAFETERIA - BREAKFAST TIME

ARNOLD (JUNIOR PRODUCTION ASSISTANT)
forks egg on a plate. He sits with JIMMY
(FILM EXTRA, ASPIRING STAR).

CONSTANCE FIELDING enters the cafeteria,
looks for a table. She has long black
hair, white blouse fitted to waist,
short skirt. Total knockout.
```

JIMMY: (*whistling*) Connie Fielding. Just started in make-up. Now there's my leading lady. What do you think?

ARNOLD (blushing) makes no response.

CONNIE looks around, holding tray with both hands. The cafeteria is full.

CONNIE: You boys mind if I sit here?

JIMMY: (*holding out his hand*) Go right ahead, the name's Jimmy. I'm an actor.

CONNIE: (*looking at ARNOLD*) And you are?

SCENE ENDS

Arnold watches the girl cross the street. She stops, now her face is reflected in a window. She fixes her hair. She turns around. Slow motion. He thinks perhaps she sees him. But he knows she sees only the shadow where a young man once stood.

He waits for time to reset. The world spins at twenty-four frames per second. He watches the girl until she's out of focus.

Now Arnold wonders about *her* story. If there's another guy too afraid to tell her how he feels, watching her the way he used to watch Constance Fielding. And maybe there's another Jimmy Cox, charming, never afraid to take a risk, the one that always gets the girl.

Something moves at his feet. When he looks it's a pigeon, matted feathers, club foot. It's turning circles on the path. Arnold tilts his head, canted framing and he thinks that in real time everything moves in one direction. No rewind.

CUT TO: NOVEMBER 1955

EXT. STUDIO PARKING LOT – LATE AFTERNOON

ARNOLD walks towards the gate.

CONNIE is standing by the office block, checking her watch.

CONNIE: (*raised voice*) Hey Arnie, you seen Jimmy? You think he had to work late again?

ARNOLD: (*shrugging his shoulders*) Maybe.

CONNIE: (*coyly*) Maybe we could get a cup of coffee?

ARNOLD: Well, I... I gotta get home to my mother... but... okay, why not.

Voice off set. JIMMY running.

JIMMY: Hey, Sorry I'm late. Thanks for keeping her company, Arn.

CONNIE looks at ARNOLD, reaches for his hand, squeezes it.

CONNIE: You could still come, Arnie.

ARNOLD: No, really. My mother's expecting me.

SCENE ENDS

Bernie G used to say, "You gotta reel 'em in with a great

opener. Think of it like a starter. Tease 'em with the first bite but leave 'em hungry."

Arnold thinks about the opener of the third movie. It starts with the promise that this is no ordinary last shift for Christian Black and Robert Walker who've been together in all three movies.

> *'Early morning in New York City. Christian looks at the photograph of Gabriella, his wife that died at the end of the second movie in what was deemed to be one of the most moving scenes in cinema.*
>
> *As he leaves the house, Christian speaks to Ben, his golden retriever.*
>
> *"See ya boy," he says. Loaded with emotional foreshadow because the audience already know that Christian Black might not come home.'*

The perfect opener.

Someone tweaks a blind at the window. Someone else rushes past him, forcing Arnold to cling to the end of his cane. The guy spins around; he's holding a pile of scripts. Pages flutter like birds about to take flight. The guy says one word, "Late."

The word you want is "Sorry," Arnold wants to say. No one has manners these days. They never treated Bernie G that way. They respected him. RESPECT in capital letters. Thirty years after the Great Bernie G died, Christian Black is a household name and Arnold Pepper is just some old guy that had something to do with it.

Inside the office block a ceiling fan whirs, whipping up air-conned air, a relic from the past, an effect that sets up the scene. Complete with girl behind desk filing her nails, chewing gum. Arnold thinks she got the *super-size* deal as she sticks out her chest, as if she's expecting someone else.

She relaxes. "Hey Arnie, it's just you," she says. "Go right ahead. They're expecting you."

"Expectations," Bernie G said, "are the seeds. And you gotta make 'em grow, Arnie Boy. They wanna be entertained. Make 'em laugh and make 'em cry. Think of the plot as the main course, what you gotta do, Kiddo, is give 'em what they ordered but with a few surprises."

Arnold passes the offices once occupied by the great legends. A corridor of dreams; built up and blown apart in the same shot. When he first pitched the idea for the third movie they thought he was crazy. They'd tried a 9/11 movie before and it flopped with a capital FLOP.

"But this is Christian Black," Arnold told them.

Fast forward:

> *'Two airplanes have crashed into the World Trade Center. The plot follows the normal structure of twists and turns and maybes. Cliffhangers that keep them pinned to their seats, teasing them with THE moment but still the hero gets up.*
>
> *But now the audience senses the resolution.'*

There's a photograph in a plastic frame hanging by the office where they're waiting for him. Arnold remembers the kid in the picture when he was a rookie, before he became a Hollywood *Star*. Some ending: they found him dead in a hotel room, drugs overdose. They all start out with dreams but dreams get too big. He thinks about Jimmy.

```
CUT TO: MAY 1956

EXT. FILM SET - EARLY EVENING

JIMMY (ACTOR, FIRST SPEAKING PART) links
arms with a blonde; she drapes herself
```

>   *all over him (giggling). They walk over
>   to ARNOLD (DIALOGUE EDITOR).*

JIMMY: Hey Arn, you coming to the party?

ARNOLD: (*looking uncomfortable*) I thought you were taking Connie out dancing.

JIMMY: Tell her something came up, will ya.

>   *DISSOLVES OUT*

"What seduces them," Bernie G once said, "is the Hollywood dream. But let me tell you, Kiddo, it's a mirage. By the time these kids get there, they're already lost. Because Arnie Boy, nothing is EVER what it seems. But if you listen good there's millions o' hard luck stories waiting in the bubbles of those champagne glasses."

Too many fucking champagne glasses Arnold thinks.

"But you got the right idea, Kiddo," Bernie G said. "Keeping it real."

Real was going home every night to the same modest home. The place he was born, the place he'll die. The place where he later nursed his elderly mother until she didn't know who he was. It took her another five years to die. No Hollywood ending. He frames the shot in his mind. The clock says 2.31 am. An old woman in a bed falls asleep. Doesn't wake up. THE END.

The door to the office is open, Arnold hears familiar voices. They're speaking in dollars.

"Arnold, good to see you. Come on in." The Chief, a small guy with round glasses called Wayne Franklin, and with him is the Executive Producer and the Assistant

Executive Producer and the Assistant to the Assistant Executive Something.

Wayne Franklin guides him towards a seat where Arnold can peep at the lot through slits in the blinds. Capture time in slices like the moving pictures from a spinning zoetrope. Same office where a decade ago he said it was time to retire. And Wayne's predecessor, a guy called Ritchie Chandelling, said, "There's this old script" and along comes the concept of the good old fashioned American hero. "All it needs," says Ritchie," is to take a contemporary guy, a modern hero and add the Arnold Pepper *old school* touch."

Wayne Franklin has a twitch, an annoying tick that Arnold can't take his eyes off as he launches into his 'why we're all here today spiel.' And the nomination for the best movie ending is…

"Okay Arnie, let's cut to the chase; which ending do we go with?"

He hears the words of Bernie G: "The ending, Kiddo, is the dessert. The taste that lingers long after the credits roll. You gotta leave 'em satisfied. But make 'em wanna eat that damn dessert in their heads again and again, Kiddo."

> 'Robert Walker is injured, in the lobby of the North Tower.
> *"I have to go back," Christian says.*
> *The audience wills him not to, because they know what happens next.*
> *Christian runs back into the stairwell. He stops. There's an injured girl. It's the moment, a second when the hero could stop to help her. All the echoes of the opener in the first movie when Christian emerges with a child in his arms. Christian takes another step. But he turns back, grabs the girl and runs into the lobby. He can't see Robert. Cracking sound.*

"GET OUT!" *someone shouts.* "GO!"
Christian takes one look back and runs. In the street, girl in his arms he keeps on running.
EXPLOSION.
The second tower collapses. BOOM. Incredible effects. Slow motion.
Camera pans out. Nothing but dust. Powerful music. Two minutes of tear-jerking emotion. But the audience still don't know.
Cut to final scene. The next day. A car pulls up at the house. The audience sees the figure in silhouette. He gets out. It's early morning. And this is the moment they'll all remember. Close up on his face.
It's Christian Black.
At the door Ben, the golden retriever is waiting.
"Hey Boy," he says. "You must be hungry."
Closing shot. Christian looks at the New York skyline in a ball of dust.
Roll music, footage of the real 9/11, a list of names of those who lost their lives.
The last name is Robert Walker, New York Fireman: Never found. Missing in Action.'

When Arnold looks back Wayne Franklin is leaning back in his seat with a pen propped between his fingers like a cigar, twitching like a horse with flies. Next to him the others wait for him to speak.

Arnold knows that whatever he's decided has to live on well after the popcorn has rotted.

Rewind.

'*"I have to go back in," says Christian.*
Christian runs back into the stairwell. He stops. There's an injured girl. It's the same, the moment when, a second in time can make all the difference.

But this time he doesn't stop. "Keep going," he says to her. "You're almost there."

Then he carries on up the stairwell. Now the audience brace themselves.

Cue EXPLOSION.

As before we see it in slow motion. Same special effects. Same powerful music. Same emotional two minutes.

Cut to final scene. A car pulls up at the house. The audience sees him in silhouette. He gets out. It's early morning. Close up. But this time it's Robert Walker. At the door Ben, the golden retriever is waiting.

"Hey Boy" he says. "He's not coming."

We see Robert Walker look at the photo of Gabriella, at the things in the house.

Now the closing shot is Robert Walker leaving with the dog. The dog jumps into his car, sits beside him. The camera pans out, view of the New York skyline in a ball of dust.

Roll list of names of those who died. Amongst them is New York Fireman, Christian Black.'

"Okay," Franklin says, leaning forwards. "So what do *you* want, Arnie?"

Arnold removes the manilla envelope from his pocket and sets it down it on the table.

"There can only be one ending," he says.

```
FLASHBACK TO: JULY 1958

EXT. OUTSIDE SOUND STUDIO - LATE
AFTERNOON

CONNIE standing with her back to ARNOLD.
He approaches, stretches out his hand
```

(hesitantly). Sensing him there, CONNIE turns around.

CONNIE: I didn't think you'd come, Arnie.

ARNOLD: It sounded important.

CONNIE: *(looking down)* I got something to tell you.

ARNOLD meets her gaze.

CONNIE: Jimmy asked me to marry him.

ARNOLD looks away.

CONNIE: Look at me Arnie. If there was something, something that a girl ought to know before she got married, you'd tell her, right?

ARNOLD looks back, lips move, no words.

CONNIE: I know about the other girls, Arnie. But I know Jimmy loves me. The things is, if there was something… someone who…

ARNOLD: *(interrupting)* Do you love him?

CONNIE: Yes. But there's this other guy only I don't know how he feels…

ARNOLD looks away

CONNIE: But if he was to say something…

> CONNIE reaches for ARNOLD'S hand, coaxes his eyes to look in hers.

CONNIE: Arnie?

ARNOLD: Good luck Connie, I hope you'll both be happy.

> ARNOLD watches CONNIE walk away.

> DISSOLVES OUT

He hears Bernie G, "Heroes don't get to grow old."

Arnold glances at Jimmy's stopped watch. The inscription says, "Good luck on your first lead role, your friend, Arn. August 2, 1958."

The movie, a low budget fireman movie was never made. Jimmy Cox and his fiancée, Constance Fielding, were in the hired car that span out of control on the road to Malibu. Too many champagne bubbles.

Time stopped on August 5th, 1958.

Arnold looks back at Wayne Franklin. Then he pushes himself out of the seat and clutches his walking cane. The envelope is unopened on the table.

"I think that's me done, Gentlemen," he says. "It's a wrap."

10 pm. Two glasses on the night table, a pot of pills and a half-read paperback, face down, spine broken. Next to the lamp is Jimmy's watch and a wedding photograph. By the window, in the shadowy light sits his wife's wheelchair. He turns, watches her sleep. Then he reaches for the light switch.

"Goodnight Connie," he says. "Sweet dreams, Kiddo."

> FADES TO BLACK

> THE END

About this story

This story received a distinction in my MA back in 2011 but has never been published – written as a personal experiment in combining forms of storytelling: the short story, film scripts and film treatments. I am a fan of the experimental and just what can be done with the short story form. In this story my intention was to use short sequences of movie script for the back story with Arnold, Connie and Jimmy and to deliberately make these quite 'ordinary' interactions compared with the other things happening in the story, i.e. Arnold's last day and the drama of the hero's ending. But actually these moments *are* the story. I liked the idea that the real hero is understated; a victim not of the Hollywood dream but happenchance. In the end it was about love – a love story that beats at the heart of everything else.

The Theory of Circles

Unplugged.
It's what you've written in your blog, dated Wednesday 7th April 5.03 pm. The very last words. It's all that's left, as if you never existed.
Not really.
Marmalade pissed up the front door of number 6.
A message Tweeted at 4.47 pm on the same day. It's ridiculously sublime and yet typical of you. Laced with humour, even to your last Tweet.

At the very edge of the day someone you've never met stares at the pages of the blog he knows intimately, and waits, the thin white edges of a polo mint dissolving on his tongue. He reloads the page, cusses a dodgy Wi-Fi connection and waits. He waits again until he realises you might just have meant it. You might just be *officially* unplugged.

Facebook status: *Undecided.* That's what you wrote twelve hours before you did it. Before that there was a brief mention that Marmalade had stalked a sock that was in Winifred's garden. In his escapades you said he'd tipped over one of Winifred's ornamental Buddhas which you noted must have been (your spelling) *ahelluva* lot lighter than it looked. You've ended with: *Why do Buddhas look like that Fred Elliot character who used to be in Corrie? I say, why do Buddhas look like that Fred Elliot character? Or perhaps,* you added, *it should be the other way round.*

No clues, then an hour later just the word undecided. Was *that* it?

And someone called Tracy J had responded with LOL. But it was too late by then – you'd already unplugged. LOL, POV, IMAO... RIP.

Everything seems so random – but it's not.
    Your words. You used to call yourself the Great Chaos Theorist. I remember the post: *Does a Polo mint obey the law of entropy when it dissolves? Experiment 1.*
    You never did say, or tell us if there was an Experiment 2 or 3.

Sunday April 4th 10.18 am. Tweet: *It just goes to show love can blossom anywhere.*
Sunday April 4th 10.17 am. Tweet: *It's official! Mohammad has moved in with Winifred. His moving in present to her: 14 pairs of size 10 slippers.*

Blog posted Monday April 1st 4.13 am: *Big Boobz kissed The Nerd on Winifred's drive. They came home late from school again – boots and coats caked in mud.*

Blog posted Monday April 1st 9.12 am: *Last night Mohammad went into Winifred's with a big bunch of purple tulips. He didn't come out for three hours, and when he did his shirt was untucked. By the way this isn't an April Fool.*

That was six days before 'The Great Unplugging.'
    That's what they're calling it – but they're still waiting for you, hoping you'll find a way back, tell them all the random *going-ons* on *The Crescent*. Send them more links to random eBooks like *Social Networking for Dodos* that you said you bought at the same time as *The Art of Reading Backwards*. But deep down, in that gut place, they all know you've gone. At first they convinced themselves you'd just

changed identity, like a snake shedding its skin. They're saying they'd find you, they'd know you anywhere.

But they don't even know your real name.

Nothing is real. Tweet dated Wednesday March 31st, 4.16 pm.

Facebook, earlier that day: *If you wait long enough everything comes full circle.*

Did this have anything to do with all the geometry references – or was it another random comment to keep them guessing?

The day before that you'd blogged that you saw Mohammad talking to Marmalade and you even saw his hand hover dangerously close to stroking his chin. You said it was funny how things changed. Like it was another golden rule of the universe. You said *nothing ever stays in the same place.* You added: *except for you.*

Saturday March 13th 10.20 am. Facebook: *Mohammad's visitors finally left: three nephews and The Aunty and at least five times as many bags as they arrived with. A ton of shoeboxes (I might have been wrong about the slipper thing.) Marmalade will miss his secret vindaloos on the front step. The Aunty seems partial to cats (might have been wrong about her eyeing him up for a curry too).*

Wednesday March 10th 2.31 am. Tweet: *A circle is a special form of ellipse that produces a closed curve.*

Monday March 8th 4.43 pm. Facebook: *Winifred took Marmalade to the vets in a picnic basket. She told the taxi driver it was on account of him having the runs. She advised* him to keep the window open. He mumbled something under his breath and looked really angry.

Tuesday March 2nd 4.12 pm. Blog Post: *The Nerd finally plucked up courage to talk to Big Boobz right outside my window. "Do you like birds?" he said. "No! You think I'm a dyke?" "No, I mean feathered twittery birds." "You mean like starlings?" "Yeah, like starlings." "You mean like the one..." "Yeah, like that one." "You mean am I like a Twitcher?" "Yeah, like a Twitcher. I mean no, not like a Twitcher, well yeah, like a Twitcher." "Fuck off." The Aunty then appeared in lime-green feathery slippers and shook her head tutting over and over like a stuck budgie. But I did see Big Boobz wink at The Nerd, then she said she was free on Saturday if he wanted to take her to the reserve but he wasn't to tell anyone. "Wear boots, it gets muddy over there," he said. Then he added, "I've got the right gear, you know the right equipment." She raised her eyebrows, "I bet you have." He blushed so hard he turned purple.*
   Later you Tweeted that *the most predictable thing about people is their unpredictability.*

Sunday March 1st 4.15 am. Tweet: *An ellipse is a smooth closed curve which is symmetric about its centre.*

Friday February 26th 11.17 pm. Blog Post: *Mohammad dug a small hole in the dirt in his front garden with a spoon – he did it when he thought no one was watching but Big Boobz would have seen him when she came out to put a black bag in the wheelie bin. And The Nerd would have seen him from his bedroom window when he was star gazing again. They would both have seen Mohammad holding something against the flat of his palm and then placing it* gently in the hole. They would have seen him spooning dirt back over it and raking it neat with his fingers. And they would have seen him cry as he read from The Koran.

Friday February 26th 5.13 pm. Blog Post: *Marmalade left a pile of starling feathers, a detached head and a line of entrails on Mohammad's front step. It reminded me of a flick painting. Do you know swear words in Urdu sound so poetic? He did a furious kind of dance too, like River Dance, only angrier. Or maybe it was a rain dance because it rained for the rest of the afternoon. I know: wrong kind of Indian.*

> Before that you'd Tweeted: *Death is the only certainty.*
> *"Are you sick?"* asked @Manic77.
> *"Are you?"* you said.

In early February you said there was a letter, an envelope on a desk that you were afraid to open. You mentioned it in a passing kind of way but it kept us guessing. Some said it was about a new job, others said you were much younger than that, that it was more like about enrolling for college, that it was the right time of year. Then someone said what if it was from the council and you were being re-housed and what would they do without their updates on *The Crescent*. But others said *The Crescent* sounded too posh to be a council estate. Or maybe it wasn't even real. People had plenty to say about that. Then someone said it had to be real and it couldn't be posh if there were foreigners living in the street. That caused a whole lot of posts about racial prejudice. You ended all that by posting: *Winifred used to be Fred.* You never said how you found out or how long you'd known but it started a whole other debate. Good save; if it was deliberate, if it was true. It stopped people talking about the letter anyhow.

Except later you did say something about an appointment, about your *condition*. But no one wanted to speculate about that. It's as if it was said by accident, a lapse, as if you'd slipped into who you really were, for a moment. You never mentioned it again, but it was there, to be sought, like a thread woven between the lines. There was a Tweet that said: *Truth is found not in what's said, but in what's not said.* You said you didn't remember where the quote came from.

Before that you posted about Big Boobz and The Nerd, how they'd been acting weird around each other since the start of the new school year. You said maybe he wasn't gay; maybe he was just shy or scared. It was like you knew something about that.

Sunday January 31st 4 pm. Facebook: *Big argument in street. Winifred caught Mohammad in her garden. He told her, "I just trying to watch bird building nest." "They all say that," she said. "Get out, you dirty old man. And stop using your hose on my cat."*

Wednesday January 20th 2.22 pm. Facebook: *The nephews have been doing odd jobs for Winifred like repairing the wall in her front garden and The Aunty is making friends with Marmalade. Hope Cat Korma isn't on the menu.*

It was around that time you noted an increase in size in the parcels arriving at number six and you treated us to elaborate descriptions of oversize boxes accompanied by eclectic wild guesses. *Far too big to be footwear* you commented once. And you told us about Mohammad's new habit of sitting in wait for the DHL man; how one afternoon in mid-January you saw him running into Winifred's garden in khaki combats with the hugest shiny binoculars you'd ever seen. You ended with the comment: *Mystery solved about big box. PERVERT.*

The week before you'd seen the DHL man try to deliver a parcel when Mohammad was out, he'd taken the car you'd remarked which was unusual. You described it as the *poomobile*. You said that's because it was brown and *looked like poo* and you said it *spluttered like a choking kangaroo*. And someone commented on your post by asking *Are you a poet?* You never did say but it led to all sorts of bizarre and wonderful rhymes. This followed the *Three Day Saga of the Missing parcel*. That's what they called it. It followed blogs that Mohammad had knocked at Winifred's to complain. *"Man from DHL say you took parcel for me,"* he'd said. *"It come when I collecting The Aunty and nephews from airport. They gave to neighbour. You give me please." "I have no idea what you're saying you silly man,"* she said. Then added, *"And don't talk to me about DHL!"*

It turned out it was The Nerd who had taken in the parcel. You said you'd seen him at his bedroom, watching the street like a peeping tom. *"Hasn't he anything better to do?"* you'd said.

Wednesday January 1st 3.17 am. Tweet: *Circles are simple closed curves which divide the plane into two regions, an interior and an exterior.*

Wednesday January 1st 3.13 am. Tweet: *Centripetal force is a force that makes a body follow a curved path. It takes a lot of force to break away.*

Thursday December 31st 12.13 pm. Tweet: *Life is too short for New Year's Resolutions.*

What did all this mean? The circle references? About life being too short? Did it have anything to do with a dissolving Polo mint? Or your condition? Or about what happened?

I have to decide what I want. This is what you said, three days before in amongst words about Christmas parties on *The Crescent* and Mohammad inviting Winifred in for a tipple, and how they both got extremely drunk and he found out something about her: something you wouldn't say. You said they'd been screaming from the back yard. *"And don't you know NOT to bring a lady lilies? Lilies! Lilies!"* she said. *"Tulips, purple tulips are for passion! Don't you foreigners know anything?"* And that's when he stood there and screamed, *"I hate your big ginger pussy!"*
Later you posted: *No one is ever who you think they are.*

Thursday November 19th 10.40 pm. Facebook: *Watched a TV show on Sky about lions in Africa. They showed a lioness that was rescued from a Russian zoo. It was the saddest thing I ever saw. They were going to move her and take her back to the wild but she died before they gave her her freedom. Animals belong in the wild: not in cages.* You wrote the same words on Twitter and on your blog.
Animals belong in the wild: not in cages.
And the next day you wrote it again.
Animals belong in the wild: not in cages.
In one post you wrote it thirty-eight times, as if it was a punishment.
Animals belong in the wild: not in cages...
For a few days it was like you'd forgotten about them all, as if life on The Crescent was passing by unobserved.

You did talk about Marmalade. You said he was the only one that was really free. *We make our own traps, you said. We look out from the inside and wait for something to happen. But it never does.*

Monday November 2nd 9.01 am. Tweet: *The circumference is the distance around a closed curve. When you stretch out the line, the distance between 2 points is always further than it looks.*

They were words for speculation, for pondering, were you talking about your life? *The Crescent*? But it was quickly forgotten when you followed it up with *Mohammad has a kipper fetish*. Then you Tweeted: *sorry meant slipper not kipper*. It spun the conjecture off in a whole other direction, centripetal but it successfully ended the speculation. It led to a lot of interesting posts about kippers.

This of course, followed three months of supposition and detailed accounts of Mohammad's strange deliveries. In one week, you reported twelve parcels. At least you stopped thinking they were ammunition, that he was a conspirator for Al-Qaeda – when in fact he was stockpiling ladies slippers, mostly feathered sling backs. *Not very effective weapons you said.*

Wednesday August 19th 10.16 am. Tweet: *Mohammad is not a terrorist; he's a pervert. They are specialists in ladies' slippers!* slipperytreats.com
Wednesday August 19th 10.12 am. Tweet: *Do flamingos live in Britain?*
Wednesday August 19th 10.10 am. Tweet: *There are pink feathers scattered all over Mohammad's front lawn*
Wednesday August 19th 10.08 am. Tweet: *Mohammad shooed Marmalade out of his house with a broom. Not sure cats understand Urdu.*

Wednesday August 19th 10.05 am. Tweet: *Just heard Mohammad screaming!*

Wednesday August 19th 10.04 am. Tweet: *Just seen Marmalade go in through Mohammad's front window*

Wednesday August 19th 9.58 am. Tweet: *Mohammad just signed for another consignment of boxes stamped SLIPPERY TREATS. Pervert.*

Tuesday August 18th 2.33 am. Tweet: *An arc of a circle is any connected part of the circle's circumference.*

Monday August 17th 11.02 am. Blog: ***WARNING*** Long Post Imminent: *There are people standing outside Mohammad's house and a bright yellow DHL van is blocking the road. A car has been blaring its horn on and off for three minutes. That's what brought Big Boobz out of her house and now she's standing in the street in cerise spotted pyjamas with her hands on her hips, exposing her midriff, her belly button glinting where the sun catches. She keeps looking at the DHL man, who looks kind of Italian and handsome, if you squint. The Nerd is at his window also watching the Italian man, with a squint. Winifred is still inspecting her wall, or what there is left of it, and the DHL man keeps shaking his head and tutting. "It's all your fault," Winifred tells Mohammad. "How it my fault?" he says. "I not driving lorry." "Well he wouldn't be here if wasn't for your parcels now would he?" The driver of the car now gets out (blond, kind of handsome without having to squint). He says, "Look I need to get to mine – number twenty-seven, can you move that thing?" "Thing? This is a state-of-the-art, Ford F-450 Super Duty E..." starts Mr DHL and now Winifred looks up from her close examining of the wall and gives him one of her hard super stares, like she's beaming lasers at him. "It's a yellow bus," she says,* "a big clumsy yellow bus. You'll have to pay for my wall." Then she looks at Mohammad who is smiling in satisfaction, "It's still your fault," she says. "Look, can you just move the van so I can get to number twenty-seven please?" the man now says. "Can't you go the other way round?" says Winifred, "We're busy here." "There's a bin lorry blocking that end." As he speaks she struts towards him towering above him; she's an enormous woman with bristly whiskers and the man seems to cower in her shadow. "Did you hear me?" she says. "We have business to sort out here." "How long are you going to be?" "How long? How long? How long is a piece of string?" "I just really need to get back to number twenty-seven." "Patience," she says, "is a virtue." And she turns with a majestic sweep of her hand and walks back towards her front door. "Where you go now?" Mohammad says, not noticing Mr DHL man wink at Big Boobz and climb back into his van. "I'm going in for a pen and paper," she says. "Insurance." "But—" Mohammad starts to speak when he sees Mr DHL is now back behind the wheel and has started the engine. "Winifred!" But she's gone and the van is already pulling away. "Winifred!" At the same time the blond man now jumps back in his car. So now the van and the car leave and that's when I see The Nerd is watching from his bedroom window with his mouth gaped open. Maybe he has a thing for Mr DHL or maybe it's Big Boobz? Maybe he's bisexual, not gay. "I suppose this is exciting as it gets around here," Big Boobz says to Mohammad and starts to walk back towards her house. Mohammad starts mumbling something about the youth of today when Winifred appears on her doorstep clutching a notebook. "They gone," Mohammad says. "I try to warn you but you go in house." She does her stare and Mohammad doesn't wait any longer but bolts to his front door and slams it shut behind him. Marmalade

appears suddenly and starts weaving around Winifred's legs. "Go away," *she says.* "Look at my poor wall." *Marmalade, as if on cue, jumps the pile of bricks and walks, bold as brass, up to Mohammad's front door where I see his tail quiver and a steaming arc of yellow piss hits the door. Winifred folds her arms across her chest and laughs. Then she rolls her head back and laughs some more. She laughs so hard she gets the hiccups. Loud belching hiccups and even Marmalade stops mid-flow to look at her. She hiccups again and holds her breath, puffs out her cheeks, goes cross-eyed. She breathes out, hiccups again cusses and goes back inside.*
Now all is quiet again on The Crescent. I see Winifred at the kitchen window drinking backwards out of a glass.
I wonder about the man at number twenty-seven.
Ps: Told you it was a long post.

You should write plays NottherealPeterAndre25 wrote in comments.
   Maybe you do? added GobScoffer1.
   You never replied. You hardly ever replied.

Friday July 31st 1.11 am. Tweet: *Do Crescents have corners?*
Friday July 31st 1.10 am. Tweet: *Someone has moved in around the corner. Rumours say a doctor.*

You didn't say a whole lot in June, it was as if you'd *unplugged* then, maybe it was a practice run. Most thought you were on holiday, others thought you were ill. The posts you did write were nonsensical, more random than usual. You talked a lot about circles. Someone said you were a mathematical genius, that you were full of answers. Others said *Yes but what is the question?* That spun us into philosophical folly until someone finally said: *Does it matter?*

Apparently the answer to that was: it did.

Sunday June 14th 1.33 am. Tweet: *A crescent is the shape produced when a circular disk has a segment of another circle removed from its edge.*

Wednesday May 20th 10.45 am. Tweet: *His name is Mohammad.*
Wednesday May 20th 9.31 am. Tweet: *Word of the day: Ethnophaulism – it means ethnic slurs.*
http://www.answers.com/topic/paki
Wednesday May 20th, 9.28 am. Tweet: *Not all Indians are from Pakistan.*
Wednesday May 20th 9.21 am. Tweet: *Is Paki an offensive word?*
Wednesday May 20th 9.15 am. Tweet: *A Paki has moved in to number 6.*
Wednesday May 20th 9.11 am. Tweet: *NOISE! NOISE! NOISE! Trucks!*

Before the Mohammad *moving in tales* you'd talked mostly about Winifred and her Buddhas. You said you thought they were breeding, multiplying at night and were now outnumbering the gnomes at number 5. You called it *The Great Gnomic Wars.* People started blogging about pixies and fairies and it started a whole other debate. Someone even ran a PVA, which is a *Population Viability Analysis* that biologists use to predict the stability and the fate of fragile populations like the Cheetah. Then someone else said you could not negate the impact of migrations on Leprechaun populations following the increase in frequency of Irish Sea crossings. By this time they'd all forgotten it had anything to do with Buddhas. But you didn't. You said *Buddhas were a sign of enlightenment*. You said to achieve this *Buddhists required abstraction from normal life* – that you said was called *ascetic practice*. You said it like it was something you envied.

There were also posts about Marmalade who you said had taken up residency in the back yard of number 6 since there was a starling's nest, guarded by a golden Buddha. And around the same time you posted about The Nerd who you said was bent. *A fruit bat* you called him and that started you on fruit Polos which you said you detested, you said the mint ones were the best. But you did point out the fruit ones took longer to dissolve. Several people put it to the test. Most commented you were right.

If you don't like fruit Polos don't suck them DavidCassidyrocks had commented.

Monday May 11th 3.07 am. Tweet: *What happens to all the holes?*
Monday May 11th 3.05 am. Tweet: *When you crush Polo mints they glow in the dark.*
Monday May 11th 3.03 am. Tweet: *140 Polo mints are eaten very second.*
Monday May 11th 3.01 am. Tweet: *An annulus (Latin 'little ring') is a ring-shaped geometric shape. It is the area between two concentric circles.*

Everything runs its course.
It's something else you said, like it was another law of the universe.

Is that what happened? To *The Crescent*? To the Polo mints? Maybe that's what will happen to the speculation; eyes will shift to blogs and Tweets and Facebook pages of other strangers. But they'll keep on checking, once in a while, seeking the randomness, hoping to find out what happened to Mohammad and Winifred – if love still blossoms, in spite of the odds. If someone else has moved into number six or if Big Boobz and The Nerd are still enjoying the antics of avian behaviour seen through Mohammad's missing binoculars. And maybe some will even ask what happened to Marmalade.

Of course I will know.

But I didn't always.

Monday May 4th 8.01 am. Blog: *Just smashed my fifty-two minute record for dissolving a Polo mint on my tongue.*

It was the first time I found you, the first thing I read, almost a year before you unplugged. An absconding mouse, a time slip into a cyber universe as if Google had plummeted me unknowingly into randomness. I was sure I'd typed 'Pogo Champions'– something just as random, in one of those nothing-better-to-do-Google-moments. And there you were, just like that, with one line that made me laugh between claims that Big Boobz's dad was having secret midnight rendezvous with the woman that used to live at number six and speculation that's why she had to move out and about The Nerd giving his phone number to the postman. Oh and something about there now being four gnomes in the front garden of number five when there used to be one and did gnomes reproduce sexually or asexually? Or were they like worms if you cut them in half?

So there I was, suddenly a part of it all.

I often wondered how the others found you. If it was by the same serendipity, all of us being sucked into it like a spinning vortex of Polo mints and mad neighbours and killer cats. Did you ever *not* accept a Facebook Friend Request?

What I didn't know then was that I was one day to become more than just a part of it. I was to be in it.

It's funny the way it happened – a cameo – a walk-on part in a play I'd stumbled into unwittingly. And there I was, a few months later, reading about myself. I never knew that our Crescent was *The Crescent*. And I still remember how you called me *kind of handsome without having to squint*. Maybe it was providence; another act of serendipity that I happened to forget my clinics appointments book that day and came back like that. And that I had to go the wrong way round around the loop, or perhaps, in hindsight the right way, if such a concept of right or wrong exists. Perhaps I had slipped into some fantastical parallel universe, the direct consequence of a refuse vehicle obstructing one end of a closed loop. *Funny how things work out*: your words, not mine. As if we'd always been there, two points on a curve, waiting to bisect.

You tell me the world is bigger than you thought it was; like a circumference stretched out. You say it as if you've just discovered the world is round, not flat, the road curved, not straight. You say you have a different view of everything. And you say that's because of me. But it took me five months to finally admit I knew who you were, as if I was trying to keep a hold of something. As if there was bird on my palm and I was afraid to let it go. But then one day I did. I opened my hand.

It was one comment on a blog: *I live at number 27.*

The beginning of the end. "Like a new moon," you said. "Everything comes full circle."

So tonight I go right back to the beginning, to where it all started, even before I found you. Seems that book on the *Art of Reading Backwards* came in quite handy in the end.

It all started, naturally, with a Tweet:

Marmalade pissed up the front door of number 6.

The Latin word for Crescent is *crescere* which means 'to grow.' It's what you said. Words spoken, not blogged or Tweeted or in a Facebook status. Just spoken. You said it when you told me your real name.

Just before you typed the word: *Unplugged.*

About this story
Published in *Unthology 3*, 2014, Unthank Books, nominated for the prestigious Pushcart Prize, 2015.

I had a lot of great comments about this one, and it was picked up in a few of the reviews. Again it's experimental, written backwards the way you scroll down a blog or Facebook post with the most recent entries at the top. I hope it makes a statement about the way we live our lives today, and this sense of the way we interact, often with strangers. Perhaps you can identify with that need that I think is within most of us but we are not quite brave enough to carry it out, and that's to… unplug.

Because Sometimes Something Happens

- 1 tablespoon olive oil
- 25g (1oz) butter
- 1 large onion, chopped
- 125g (4½ oz) leeks, rinsed and sliced
- 280g (10oz) parsnips, peeled and chopped
- 400g (14oz) carrots, peeled and chopped
- 1 large potato, peeled and chopped
- 900ml (1 pint 12fl oz) vegetable stock
- 4-5 tablespoons semi-skimmed milk (optional)
- Salt, black pepper and freshly grated nutmeg
- 2 tablespoons chopped parsley

Monday morning. No rain. Clear sky.
    Soup.
    It's the kind of morning Mother used to call 'crisp'.
    Crisp like leaves scuttling along Church Lane. Crisp like croutons in a bowl before they sog. Crisp like salt and vinegar.
    Walkers.
    Has to be Walkers.
    I must add them to the shopping list.
    It's the kind of morning that reminds me of Mother. The kind of morning for making winter soup.

    1. Heat the oil and butter in a large saucepan. Add the onion and leeks and cook, stirring, over a medium heat, for 4-5 minutes until soft. Add the parsnips, carrots and potato and cook, stirring, for 2-3 minutes.

The house would fill up with soup.

The smells would waft up from the kitchen. They'd coat the walls of the bedroom; drift along the drafty hallways. Like a spell; a spell cast to chase away winter greyness. Before the soup, there was always greyness – like the past was a place in monochrome. A place where Mother would stand at the window; and get stuck. A place where she'd wait… for *him,* for the next time, for something to happen.

It seemed as if the days folded themselves into one another. A mass of tangled bedsheets. Mother always in her dressing gown.

Until one day something did happen.

1980.

The first time Mother made winter soup.

I stand at the window, trace a crack along one of the panes; watch a line of steam rising from my tea.

Weak, Earl Grey, milky, insipid tea.

It's how I like it. How Mother liked it.

I wonder if something will happen today.

I stare at the back yard. Not as cluttered as Doreen's. Doreen over the road. Doreen who collects 'stuff'. Lots and lots of 'stuff': bin bags, boxes, carrier bags. I look at Mother's vegetable patch with its runner bean wigwams and its neatly sowed row of cabbages. It used to be the only bit of the house with any order. Not that it's much different now to when Mother was alive.

I think about carrots. Carrots, parsnips, leeks, onions, spuds.

All home grown – which is just as well; I've not left the house since 1995.

It was the same day Bet Gilroy left *Coronation Street.*

Simply Red was number one.
I found Mother hanging in the bedroom.

I lean over the gas stove and gently stir with a wooden spoon. I look at the pile of carrots on the chopping board.

All I did was go out for milk. Many times I have told myself not to cry over *bought* milk.

Red-top, homogenised – none of that skinny fat-free nonsense.

Mother must have had it all planned. Sent me across town to the new Tesco because the corner shop always ran out of milk by 3 pm. All the way to Tesco while she—

S-n-a-p.

I chop the last carrot, add it to the pile of veg and then scrape them off the chopping board into the pan of oil where onions and leeks sizzle.

Doreen goes to the corner shop for me now – because you can't 'home grow' everything. You can't home grow ketchup.

Or Walkers crisps.
Or angel cake.
Or Nutella.
Or newspapers.

I picture Mother, knelt down, knees pressed into the *Crompton Gazette*. She always sent me for it, never read it. I read it for her. *Anything?* No, Mother. Nothing interesting.

Good for keeping the knees dry, Giles. Yes Mother.

Good for: sowing, weeding, digging.

Sometimes she'd sing theme songs off the TV, *Cagney and Lacey* was her favourite. Singing helps the vegetables grow she'd say.

But mostly she'd hum to them. She never did that – sing or hum or dig before 1980.

What I remember most about Mother was how she got stuck in a loop. Like the time she said there was a man in the moon and don't you see its face right there, Giles. Where? There. See? No. There. Where? Oh for goodness sake, Giles. There, see it? Yeah.

Of course I didn't see it – but I didn't want to be stuck in the same conversation.

And then in school we learned about the men who landed on the moon. I'd been five, I didn't remember it. So I said: so there was a man in the moon? Cue blank stare… so I added I wonder what part of the face he landed on? And she said face? What do you mean face? You said there was a man in the moon and that the moon has a face. Don't be silly, Giles. You did. You said there was always a half we never see, like the moon has two faces. I said that? Yeah. Didn't. Did. Giles, it's the moon, it's made of rock and it doesn't have any faces. Yeah. It's made of rock and it doesn't have any faces.

It was another conversation I didn't want to get trapped inside.

It all changed after the soup.

Happy sounds wafted up from the kitchen. And colourful soupy smells. But before that, it seemed her life was a repeating cycle of cigarette burns and bruises.

Until he was gone.

I turn back from the window; glance at the calendar. Two more sleeps then I turn the page for December. Doreen loves Christmas; she'll buy more stuff: sparkly stuff and bits of tinselly twinkly stuff and she'll try to put it in my kitchen and create some 'festive cheer' she says. I let her do it, you can't argue with Doreen.

You should leave the house, Giles. Yeah, Doreen, I should.

You should start clearing the stuff, Doreen. *Yeah, Giles, I should.*

We never do – as if something centripetal stops us breaking free from ourselves.

I think about the Christmas tree under the stairs. White. Green box. A bag of red baubles. She'll be telling me to fetch it soon. *Where's your Christmas spirit, Giles?* She has to ask a few times before I eventually concede. I never told her how until *he* was gone there were no Christmas trees. No colour. And how the cupboard under the stairs had a whole other use. Or about the shouting or the *other stuff*.

And definitely no one would wrap you in tinsel and make you sing 'The Twelve Days of Christmas' and do that silly jig thing she loves. Or watch cheesy Christmas movies and fight over the purple ones in the Quality Street.

I move to the front window; peer across at number 7. Lights on. Doreen'll be up. She'll be eating eggs: soft boiled, runny, two of them. With white bread cut into soldiers. I look over at the row of terraces; the new moon like a thin fingernail perched on the edge of the crisp new day, before someone spoils it.

I think about my telescope, still in the shed in its box. After Father was gone I'd stare at the moon and I'd plant vegetables in sync with the lunar phases because it said you could do that in the book Mother bought me from Oxfam. 32p. The price is still there; scribbled in pencil on the inside cover.

I used to picture the water being dragged up through the soil as if the man in the moon had a giant straw. But I didn't like to think about that.

Mother had her own lunar cycles. 'Loony cycles' I told Dr Woods once. He didn't even smile. There were a lot fewer of those, or as Dr Woods preferred, 'episodes' after *he'd* gone. But they never stopped. Not completely. Not forever.

I pour stock over the carrots and the leeks; and the onions and potatoes; stand over Mother's big pot while the steam rises. It smothers my face; like a pillow. I inhale the soupy smells until I can't breathe; until I have to turn away.

When I think about it now, Mother was like the moon, part of her face always turned away, always hidden. Scarves, hoods, fingers. *Go for the paper, Giles. I don't feel well.* She must've thought I never saw what she hid, the dark side.

But that stopped when Father was gone.

We were never allowed to talk of him. Not even to Dr Woods, *especially* not to Dr Woods, who filled her prescriptions that sometimes worked and sometimes didn't when she forgot to take them, and she had to 'go away' for a bit. They assumed Father was still about and we never said.

No one has to know, Giles. No Mother. *No one has to know what we did.*

I listen to the soft simmer of finely chopped vegetables and wonder if they scream as they start to boil.

2. Pour in the stock, bring to the boil, then simmer for 20-25 minutes until all the vegetables are tender.

I hear the waking up sounds on Church Lane: the dog at number 4 yelping to be let in and it's ages before someone does, the clink-clink that bottles make when they're dropped into the recycling, balls being slapped against concrete, and mothers shouting *Don't be late for school!* I don't remember my mother even caring if I went to school. Of course I went – but who calls a kid Giles? Not someone from the East End. It always ended in tears. Bullying is not a new thing. But I could handle *them* – they were just kids.

I see the neon blur of Mr Winters' coat as he leaves number 5; he walks with big manly strides to the end of Church Lane where Doreen says a van picks him up. What kind of van? *Dunno. Why?* Just wondering. *A white one I think. Does it matter?* No. She says he works in construction, talks with an accent. What accent? *Dunno, up north.* Like a Corrie accent? *Yeah. Well no. A bit like it. More like Liverpool.* Oh.

Mother always said I was nosey. I took her place at the window when she was gone – standing, watching, wondering about people, and hoping something would happen.

Except… it already had.

The people come and go, I've seen them all: young couples who get pregnant and then get pregnant again and then they have to move to a bigger house somewhere else. Foreigners: Polish mostly, Indian, West Indian, students, druggies, old people… No one seems to stay long: just passing through. Doreen talks to them all.

She's been teaching the little Polish girl from number 10 – English – because that's what she used to be. I don't mean English, she still is English, I mean an English teacher; at Crompton Comp, before they *had to let her go* and she started to collect the stuff. Although she told me once she started collecting the stuff before that, when—

When?

She gets stuck sometimes, but not the way Mother did – mid-flow. As if the truth lies in the space that comes after the unfinished sentences.

When?

Secrets make people get stuck… and stay inside… and hoard things.

When, Doreen, love?

When George died.

That's her son. He was eight. Knocked down by a car outside her old house. 1977. The night of the Queen's Silver Jubilee. He was wearing a fireman's outfit, refused to change after the children's street party. She left him sleeping. Forgot to check on him. Her husband left her after that. Grief can do that. Change people. And so can guilt.

She doesn't like to talk about it just as I never like to talk about Mother. Or Father. Doreen came to Church Lane after 1980 but she was here the day Mother sent me to Tesco for red-top milk.

First time she'd spoken to me properly. Not that I remember words. She stood in the doorway after the ambulance had left... and the black van had left... and Dr Woods had left with his *I'm so sorry, Giles. I can get you the name of someone to talk to.* But I had Doreen; she was someone to talk to after they'd all left.

I remember standing in the hallway and her pulling me into her and holding me and my arms hanging limp at my sides. She smelled of sponge cake. And there we stood until she said she'd make tea and how did I like it and she said she wasn't sure what I meant by 'insipid' and did that mean lots of that red-top milk and I said yes and then I said no, on second thoughts...

She came every day after that.

Went to the funeral for me so she could tell me who turned up.

You ought to go, Giles. You might regret it. No.

No one else was there except for Doreen and Mother's older brother, William, who was the only one who stayed in touch when she started to have her episodes. And a handful of people from the church who come because the vicar asks them to. No one came back for cake or egg sandwiches or tea. No one did anything. No one knew what to do, or say because no one wants to think about how a person looks when they hang themselves and the police have to cut them down or how loud the thud is when they land on a wooden floor. No one wants to think about that.

Bodies are heavy without a soul inside them. I never told anyone that.

Of course, Mother already knew.

I prod a carrot; the blade sinks into the soft flesh. I spear a spud; to be sure before I click off the gas. The steam has coated all the windows. I wipe along the crack with the sleeve of my green cardigan, gaze out. The vegetable patch is looking so verdant.

> 3. Transfer to a blender or food processor and process until smooth. Return to the saucepan and pour in a little milk to thin, if needed. Season with salt, pepper and nutmeg, then stir in the parsley.

I often think that after they cut Mother down maybe she would have been a whole lot lighter.
Unburdened.
Free.
But was she?
Maybe the weight of all that guilt never really leaves.
It's not the same for me. It wasn't me who—
I was just a kid.
Sixteen.
All I did was—
Help.
To move him.
He was heavy.
It wasn't her fault.
I mean if she hadn't, he would have—

You know.

Doreen doesn't know about Father. No one does.

When people came asking we said we didn't know where he was. Only two came anyway: someone from the factory where he worked; don't remember who the other one was. Just that Mother stood at the kitchen sink drying the same spot on the soup bowl over and over while she looked out at the vegetable patch. *He left,* she said. *I don't care where he went. He left us. Good riddance.*

Doreen will be over soon for her shopping list – and for soup; she likes Mother's winter soup. She slurps. *I don't.* Do. *Don't.* Okay you don't. Then we laugh and she slurps louder and I think about what kind of mother she must have been to George, a fun one – caring – nice – and the kind of teacher she was – and that when you look at someone you never really know what's inside them.

All they see are bin bags, boxes and carrier bags.

All they see of me is a face at a window.

No one knows anything – do they?

Maybe one day Doreen *will* clear the stuff.

Maybe one day I *will* leave the house.

Maybe one day I'll get the Christmas tree out early. Surprise Doreen.

A lemon sun lifts over the Church Lane roof tops and the moon is barely a whisper now. The cabbages look ready: crisp. Like the day.

The vegetable patch is blooming.

I think how sometimes nothing happens. And sometimes it does.

And when it does, some secrets are best kept buried.

4. Reheat gently. Best not served cold.

About this story
Placed third in Leicester Short Story Prize, 2019, published in *Leicester Writes Anthology*, Volume 3, June 2019.

This started life as a chapter from the current work-in-progress novel and I developed it into a short story – which is unusual because I generally do it the other way round, developing short stories into longer works. Why did I do this? I was inspired by a competition to write something that used food.

When the Bees Die

If you want to keep a secret, you must also hide it from yourself.
                                    George Orwell, 1984

```
When the time comes - run.
```

You can have it all: the perfect body, the perfect home, the perfect life – even if you don't want it.

Slogans beat out time as her feet slap rain-drenched pavements. Puddles reflect the latest *must-have* items – images floated over the city in giant neon arcs. Between the pictures – the words – perfectly timed with the blinks. The subliminal messages of modern living.

Think it – and it's yours. Take this supplement and you will live forever.

It's all a ruse.

Nothing is perfect. No one lives forever.

Rain splashes her fake Reeboks as she turns the corner.

No tracker, no chip, no phone. She no longer exists. Because if she did – they'd know.

These days they can track everything – even your thoughts. *Especially* your thoughts.

She remembers something her dad said before she went to marketing school.

Once they get inside your head, Ashleigh, they can make you do anything.

Oh come on, Dad…

Just you wait and see, Honey.

Now her dad is missing.

No one calls her Honey.

And all the bees are dead.

* * *

Ashleigh turns the corner.

She likes the feel of the cobbles; hard under her feet. She tugs at the zipper of her favourite hoodie: a gift from her mom. They try to make you stay inside: **work out** at home, **work** at home and the part they don't tell you – **go quietly mad** at home.

Sometimes you just need air.

It's what she used to tell Mark – before they got to him too.

Nothing like the feel of a real road – not the rubber of treadmills. Nothing like the wind in your face – not the stuff they pump out.

Don't you ever just… wanna go outside?
No Ash. No one has to.
Why? Because the carcinogens are gonna get you?
What-ever, Babe.
Maybe it's what they tell you to stop you going outside?
…God she hates it when he calls her 'Babe'.
Stop acting crazy, Ash.
Crazy? She hates that word even more. He knows that. And he knows why.

Anyway, something else gets you if you stay inside – only she never said that part.

Like thinking the *crazy* things. How it was thinking the *crazy* things that made her quit her job. It was thinking the *crazy* things that made her do what she did. All that blood.

And it was thinking the *crazy* things that led her here – to this moment – and what she is about to do.

She crosses into the side street, looks up at the latest fancy new *ultimate in city living* apartment blocks – *so luxurious you'll never want to leave* and she heads east towards the university, where her dad used to work. It's nothing but an empty shell now; one that casts a long shadow. Like the city wall. They used to say it was to stop the bad people getting in but now she thinks it's to stop the good people getting out.

Rules are made to be broken, as she used to tell Mark. He thought it made her like her mom – she saw it on his face. He used to watch her. She should never have told him.

Mark was the perfect match on an internet dating site. And for a while she really thought he was 'perfect', even if he was the result of an algorithm. *They* choose who you date, who you marry, who you make babies with – only they try to tell you not to do that; they implant a chip that stops you doing that, that feeds you birth control hormones. There won't be enough food they tell you, the population needs to be controlled. There was an advertising campaign about that.

The year before they were telling you where to go to make 'perfect' babies.

They can brainwash you into believing anything – all they gotta do is make you think it's your own decision. Her dad was right.

See it or hear it three times and they've got you.

The motto of modern marketing.

The matches at **findaperfectmatch.com** are supposed to last forever. The site claims *almost* 100% success.

Now she knows what the 'almost' means.

Anyway, who wants perfect? And who wants to live forever?

She used to think Mark was the *bees knees*, if bees have knees: it's an expression her dad used to use. Apt. Given that he was head of The Bee Project. *Was.* Sometimes she thinks he's like one of those files.

What do you mean one of those files? Mark'd said.

Deleted.

Don't be stupid, Ashleigh, he didn't get deleted, he took a break.

Where? Nowhere-on-Sea?

Sabbatical.

That was six months ago. But no one goes on sabbatical these days. People don't just leave, Mark.

Except it turns out they do.

Mark was gone three weeks later.

Packed up his things and removed himself from her life four months ago. 'They' became the blip on a dating site statistic.

The next day she was bombarded with ads from another online dating company. That's when she realised they were listening to everything – that's when she knew she had to pull the plug. But what if they already knew what she'd done?

You could do it fast, like pulling off a Band-Aid or you could do it slowly – app by app. She imagines herself like a dot, a pixel that fades slowly… to nothing.

Like her mom.

Only she did her leaving brain cell by brain cell.

As Ash listens to the pound of her trainers on the wet city streets she thinks about the last app she deleted. The screen is always on only she can't see it anymore – it has to be that way. Better that way her dad would say. There'd be an alert for everything: heart rate, number of breaths, every time she turned the kettle on (if she remembered what a kettle was for) or opened her bowels. Her mom is a hamster in a cage. What kind of life is that? She told them that too. She doesn't remember when. What kind of life, huh?

It's okay, Honey. It will be okay, sweetheart.

They say Alzheimer's is hereditary, caused by the build-up of amyloid; the gene sits on Chromosome 21. She doesn't know if she has the gene. Only her dad knows that. He's the geneticist – *better not to know,* he said, *there's nothing anyone can do. The technology hasn't gotten there yet.*

She read that if you have the gene you have 100% chance of developing the condition.

No 'almost' about that one.

They were sat in their old house – maybe ten years ago – TV re-runs of shows they sent direct to your TV, nothing with any violence, nothing that made you think for yourself. He handed her the book. She didn't read it all. Mom was sleeping in her favourite chair. Facing the ocean, a lemon blanket draped over her. God she misses the ocean.

They can control everything else, why not the genes, Dad?

His eyes stayed on the TV screen. Some Hallmark crap.

Dad? Unless—

A flicker, a slight tilt of the head.

Unless they already can? Is that it, Dad? Can they?

No, Honey.

But he was never a good liar.

They can, can't they? Then they can help Mom? Then why don't they try to—

They both looked over at her; she looked so normal, as if Chromosome 21 was sleeping as she did.

She remembers the small twitch in his left eyebrow when he turned back to her. She remembers his words: she thinks them now.

They know how to switch on the genes, Honey... like who would want to do that? *But they don't know how to switch 'em off. Once it starts, there's no way back.*

He was the one who later said not to look – *it's not her, Honey. She's already left us. Remember... think about who she was, not who she is – or isn't.*

The rain eases to a fine mist; it coats everything. She turns west, takes all the 'secret' backstreets. She used to run the same route every morning, testing the air, like treading water; how far can you push the boundaries? She didn't plan to run the same route every morning but it's like fighting human will: routines get established, that's what they rely on: buy this brand; bank with this bank (when money was a real thing). Never break the rules – believe everything they tell you.

But sometimes you have to prove you're not like everyone else.

She wonders about the people beyond the checkpoints and the city wall, people living outside the law. Maybe it's all hype; it might be Disneyland out there. She used to imagine when people disappear they went to a magical place, just out of reach. All you had to do was find a way in. Like with her mom. She remembers visiting the old Presbyterian Church way across town; she doesn't know when it was. Most of the churches are gone now. This one had beautiful stained glass. She remembers how she'd prayed to a God she didn't know was even there, pressed her hands tightly together like the harder she pressed the more God would listen. She prayed for her mom to be safe now. And for her dad to save all the bees. And she thinks now how she'd add that she so wants heaven to be a real place. A magical place beyond the city walls. Not just some ideal they tell you when people leave – or die – or disappear – or… take a 'sabbatical.'

She wants to believe her dad is still alive.

Ashleigh has no detectors on.
There are no cameras on this route.
She is doing exactly what she was told to do.
Just like she planned.
There's a place where you can get beyond the walls; where you can pass go. Where they don't stop you. That's

what the message said. But if you do – you can't come back.

She thinks about her mom.

She used to run as far as the city wall and wonder what would happen if she kept on running but she'd get to the checkpoint and turn back. Maybe because her mom was still there, someplace, no one was allowed to visit.

I don't know what's real, Ash? her mom used to say to her – in her more lucid moments: rare moments snatched between all the others.

Love is real, Mom, she'd tell her. This. Right now. This moment. This is all that counts.

And they'd hug her until her mom had forgotten who she was again.

Ash looks ahead at the checkpoint.

She used to dream about what was beyond the walls…

But today she'll know.

She remembers her dad working long hours in the lab when she was growing up; and all those months away in a clinic in New York. He'd bring her back gifts: snow globes and one time a small statue of the Empire State Building. But it wasn't gifts she wanted. Take me with you, Dad. She used to think he loved the bees more.

I wish I could, Honey. He said what he was doing was important work for the government – but she knew he was *really* doing it for the bees. His first great love: he kept bees with his father, growing up in Milwaukee. He used to talk about it all the time.

Without the bees, there'd be no pollination. Without that there'd be no crops. *It's like dominoes* he said; *one falls down and everything else follows. In the end everything will die.*

So your job is to save the world?
Yeah, something like that.
Like a super hero?
He laughed. How she misses that laugh.
All you have to do is save the bees, Dad.
Yeah.
Only it was never that simple, was it?
And nor was that quite true.

`When the time comes – run.`
She slows down and ducks into the doorway of an old warehouse. She can be arrested for going outside, for taking a run. Mustn't let them see her.

Her first memory was five years old, a vacation in the south of France, the three of them, her, Mom (before she got sick), Dad… the bees. He taught her everything: about the colony; its social structure, the intricacy of the honeycomb, the Queen Bee and the Royal jelly, the drones, the honey that she used to help him collect so carefully from the hives. *Always be thankful, bow your head and thank 'em for the honey. Especially the Queen Bee.* And he made her put on the special clothes, like dressing up. She would curtesy for the Queen Bee and they'd both laugh. It must be great being that important she told them.

Above all else you gotta respect the bee.
She remembers the feel of his gloved hands over hers: *be careful. Honey. Don't want to get stung. Like this…* He told her once: *You can learn a lot about how to build a society from the honey bee. If I had to start civilisation again – I'd do it like the bees; build a colony and work together…* And the part that stayed with her: *All we need is one strong Queen Bee, to start over.*

Why would you need to start over?

She wasn't sure what she saw in his eyes when she said that.

Man is the one you can't trust, Honey.

Of course she didn't understand it then.

She remembers the last time she saw him; he seemed so... *normal*. Or maybe when she thinks about it that's just what she told herself. He'd seemed agitated for months; thinner, the job was getting to him. And there was the worrying about Mom. She'd just gone into that place. *Don't look anymore, Honey.* He said she had to trust him on that. *It's not healthy...*

But who *do* you trust?

Does he trust the government now?

She already knows the answer to that.

All we need is one strong Queen Bee, to start over.

She knew something was wrong when he hadn't returned her call that Saturday morning. He'd never do that. No one had seen him at the university. Someone she didn't know told her The Bee Project was in trouble. What did they mean The Bee Project was in trouble?

His apartment looked the same; like it was waiting for him to walk back into his life.

She tried to tell Mark he would never have just left. He would never do that. The cops said they'd speak to the university. The university told them he was on sabbatical. The cops told her the same thing; maybe you should've talked to your father. She did talk to him and that's how she knows he would never just leave.

Her dad told her once how bees find their way home using landmarks; flying circuits above their heads that most people don't even notice. It's what she used to imagine – him trying to get home and then one time she wondered if that's what her mom's memories were like – like the bees – just trying to find a way to land. Until one day it was too late.

Lost.

Memories.

Moments.

Time.

Her mom.

Her dad.

People leave all the time they said. Your dad's not lost if he chose to go.

Now the university building is empty. The bees are dead. Ashleigh no longer exists.

It's raining harder now. The ends of her brown hair drip along the back of her neck, shivery pinpricks that pucker flesh. She skips off the pavement to run around a dead rat.

She feels the sting of the rain on her arm, the scar still red at the edges; and she presses on. Can't turn back now. She remembers all the blood. What she did.

```
Run, Ash. Keep running. You're almost
there.
```

She has to know.

She has to know what's out there.

All she knows is that a voice talks to her inside her head, a voice that says: `Trust no one.`

Sometimes she thinks it's her dad's voice but he would call her 'Honey' and sometimes she thinks it's her mom, but she can't even remember her voice. And other times she thinks it's one of them, still inside her, like someone has implanted a chip inside her head, maybe to replace the one she cut out of her arm.

She thought she'd never stop the blood.

Sometimes she feels nothing except for the buzz that

grows louder, telling her to keep on running.

    `Don't let them get you…`

    Is that what it was like for her mom?

    They used to find her wandering, bare feet, sometimes in just her dressing gown. She used to mumble how everyone was after her.

    And in her lucid moments: *Don't be like me, Ash, don't be like your crazy mom.*

    Don't be silly, Mom. You're safe now.

    But was she?

Why don't they just stop using pesticides, why don't they stop killing the bees? She remembers asking her dad when she was a kid.

    His face had gotten that look; that sad distant *you are so young* look. He had reached out; pulled her towards him until she felt the warmth of his breath tickle her cheeks. *I wish it was that simple* he said. *Sometimes you run and run and never get anywhere.*

    Like on a treadmill, Dad?

    Yeah, just like that, Honey, like on a treadmill. And one day you discover there is no Noah; there is no Ark – we will never save all the animals.

    But you said you only had to save one, Dad?

Ashleigh used to imagine a world without bees; how quiet the air would be. As she turns onto the main road towards the checkpoint she thinks about the city with no buzz. The buzz is inside of her now.

    She feels the hardness of the cobbled wet pavements; lifts her head into the rain, runs towards the checkpoint in her fake Reeboks; the giant rainbow slogan in the air about her head. *Our shoes make you feel like you're running on air.*

She pictures her mom; thank God she doesn't know what's happening. She runs a hand across the dome of her belly. Nothing like belonging to someone – or a mother's love. There are tears stinging her eyes; wetting her cheeks. I'm sorry, Mom.

And thank God Mark doesn't know what she did. She cleaned away the blood – hid the cut with her sleeve. Told him how much she loved him. She said it three times. *I love you too, Babe.*

```
Almost there.
```
You can learn a lot from the way bees live, Honey.
All we need is one strong Queen Bee, to start over.

The checkpoint is straight ahead. She sees the outline of someone.

It can't be?
Is that you, Dad?
She doesn't look back.
She keeps on running.

March 17th 2044

27-year-old, Ashleigh Davies, daughter of renowned Head of The International Bee Project, Professor Stuart Davies, has been diagnosed with sudden early-onset Alzheimer's. The genetics of the disease are complex and it is extremely rare in someone so young. Yet another example, the government claims, of the accelerant effects of environmental pollutants. The condition causes memory loss, confusion and mood changes, manifesting as a decline in the ability to think and reason clearly and in some severe case can cause delusions and hallucinations. Until last year Ashleigh was an apparently healthy young woman who liked to run and was employed in marketing for a sportswear giant. Grief was probably also a contributing factor in her mental decline. Mother, Rosemary Davies, died three years ago aged 66 but her daughter was never able to process it, believing she was still alive somewhere. Mrs Davies was diagnosed with Alzheimer's at the age of 57. Ashleigh has now been moved to a newly opened state-of-the-art live-in facility where she is the first to be selected for a trial with tracking software that allows her to be monitored 24/7. This utilises a phone app and will be rolled out to more patients over the next few years if the trial is successful. Sadly Ashleigh's condition is not expected to improve.

This news comes just days after Professor Davies, currently on sabbatical, announced his retirement. This follows the news that The Bee Project has been deleted after reports confirmed that the Honey Bee is now officially extinct.

About this story
Written on a writer's retreat four years ago, but developed only recently, this comes from my interest in how the mind works. You will see a lot of exploration of 'broken minds' in this collection. Until I put them together I had not realised how much my writing explored that. I have recently read *Still Alice* that explores early-onset Alzheimer's. I

am also a fan of dystopian literature and fascinated with bees and this idea that the world ends if the bees die – although that is not quite true. I started out with a simple idea of something set in the future and about bees – and *this* is what happened.

Four Minutes in April

Corners of the newspaper flutter. Black and white faces of astronauts stare out. A telephone cord twists around a finger.

She hangs up before her momma speaks again.

The boy has his back to her. Simon and Garfunkel play on the radio. She thinks how she has her own troubled waters.

He speaks her name; he's the only one who shortens it to 'Mel'. Her real papa called her 'My State Flower', 'course he's long gone, lost in the whispers, shut behind the closed doors.

He has blue eyes – the boy – not her papa. The breeze drops. The silence a line waiting to be crossed. She'd said *yes, she's ready, only her momma's due home from the early shift... but... if she's late... if...*

He must know only her momma calls the house.

Their fingers touch. Her skin chocolate brown against his blush – but where the tips meet they are the same. Only that's not how folks think. Two years ago a preacher was shot dead in Memphis for *having a dream* and now there's a white boy standing in front of her.

The right time – the right boy – the right moment.

She watches him walk across the kitchen in his Levi's, watches him pull the door closed, watches him draw the curtains across. It's supposed to be a time for freedom – that's what the marches were about – but nothing is free. Everything comes at a price. They talked about the preacher the next day in school. They were in school when they heard about her brother: half-brother. The half makes all the difference.

In the bedroom, four faces look out from a photograph: three sets of brown eyes. One of them belongs to the man who raised her. It's not all he raised. He's gone too.

The troubled waters end. The new number one plays.

On the bedroom door are her half-brother's carved initials. They shared the room before *the trouble*. That's what her momma calls it, *the trouble* like she measures time before and after the police came to their door. She wonders if he carves 'JJ' into the walls of his cell.

She lets her boy ease her slowly onto the bed. Grandmomma said, "Camellia, you'll know when the time's right, honey." It was one of the last things she said to her. She was fourteen; standing in the hospital looking into that sweet lined face not knowing it was the last time.

Momma tells her not everything that looks sweet tastes sweet.

Three years later her boy is here and the time *is* right. But if she is doing nothing wrong, why does it feel like she is?

Their lips touch. The voice on the radio sings: "Let it be".

– This is mission control at Houston: we've just had loss of signal from Honeysuckle, Apollo 13…
`- Begin radio blackout`

Gabriella tells herself she's dying. She's not – it's the baby. Only it can't be coming. Not yet. *Can it?*

A line of white light bleeds onto nicotine walls. The air smells of excess. The window is propped open by a beer can, the curtain flaps. Clock says 1 pm. Almost over. She wishes she'd told her momma there was a baby. She wishes she'd told *him*. She pulls herself up, sweat drips along black skin.

She cries out: for a baby she didn't want and now she does; for a baby that hasn't moved.

Maybe she's being punished for getting knocked up by a boy three years younger. Punished for what *he* did.

A distant siren wails. Blood tumbles onto unwashed sheets.

– About thirty seconds to go for black out.
– About ten seconds now. We will attempt to contact Apollo 13 through one of the ARIA aircraft.
– Continuing to monitor; this is Apollo Control, Houston.
```
- 5 seconds to end of radio blackout
```

A white line crosses black.

The doctor instructs them to go again. The nurse stands with her back to them: counts swabs. She hears a chest being pumped, forced lifeless moans, the cracking of a rib.

The man has been in the ER for seventeen minutes; in cardiac arrest for thirty-one. She has seen death a million times, but she has never had someone she knows wheeled into her ER. He'd been picking trash in Memorial Park. The cops call him John Doe: Caucasian.

But she knows his real name.

– Listening for Apollo 13.
– We have a report that ARIA-4 Aircraft has acquisition of signal.
– Odyssey Houston standing by. Over.
```
- Still in radio black out - listening for
Apollo 13
```

The doctor records time of death. The ER is eerily silent

except for the crackle of a radio in the waiting room. Then:
– *"Houston 13."*

They have never heard cheering before in their ER.

Blood stains two sets of sheets: taints pure white cotton in a house in Birmingham, Alabama, where a young girl scrubs her secret away before her momma comes home.

The other set wraps a baby boy in an ER. Took him a whole four minutes to breathe. She names him after his father – Joe – last name Johnston: a fifteen-year-old boy, still a minor, incarcerated in the state of Alabama for killing three white boys. But Joe Johnston didn't do it. In the state he is deemed too young to drink. He is not too young to make a baby. And he is not too young be on death row.

It took four minutes for a white judge to decide.

Another sheet covers the body of a John Doe in an ER where a nurse dials her daughter's number to say she's leaving work now. The phone rings out. As she steps outside the hospital she pictures the face of the man on the gurney; the only man she ever loved. Forbidden by her momma. She knew him from his green eyes – like their daughter's.

She looks up, wonders if the weatherman has forecast rain.

- End radio black out. Prepare for splashdown.

About this story
Winner in City Writes Short Story Competition, 2018. I love the idea of taking real moments in history and using them in a story

Paper Chains

The things which are seen – are temporal, but the things which are not seen – are eternal.
Corinthians 4:18

The little boy hippedy hops his way along the high street; his grandfather's clasp weakening and readjusting itself, like skin to skin Morse code – *not so fast – slow down – what's the hurry?*

But there's always hurry with a six-year-old.

His teacher wants them to make Christmas paper chains.

He loves Christmas paper chains.

He has already told his teacher what colour he wants to make the Christmas paper chains.

He likes the way the different colours feel.

"But they feel the same," the teacher told him. "You can't *feel* colour, Ben."

But his dad taught him you can. His dad showed him how blue feels.

As the old man, a wilted poppy still in his lapel, opens and closes bony fingers over the smallness of Ben's warm fingers, he feels them slip; feels the space open up; feels the skipped-beat of an *almost let go*.

It happens as the number 66 rushes past with its judder and its rattle and its startled faces at misted windows. Faces thinking in swear words: *Oh my God – did you see that little boy?* And the thing they only *think* they see: a soldier standing on the pavement pulling the little boy back, but it's so fleeting they tell themselves they don't see it.

And now the old man wonders what he'd say to Ben's mother if his fingers did go slippedy slip. It's the kind of thing he's read in the news. It's why he's stopped reading the news. If Gertie was still here she'd tell him *Albert, you worry too much.* But she's not here, is she.

He doesn't remember worrying like this about his Susan. Maybe that's where he went wrong. She slipped away so slowly he never felt her go.

He holds on tighter, like a pinch.

"It hurts, Grandad."

"Yes, it does, Son. Yes it does."

The old man mutters until the bus has turned at the lights. Ben's step quickens, his tongue is pushed to one side as he makes little determined grunts, the way he remembers his daughter doing at the kitchen table trying not to colour over the lines. And later, trying not to step on the cracks and Gertie saying *is that normal, Albert?* But how do you know what's normal?

A last afternoon walk – is that normal? A last afternoon walk with your wife when you don't know it's the last afternoon walk.

Walking your grandson to school like you do every day – skipping to avoid puddles and cracks that weren't there yesterday and wondering if he will end up like his mother?

Sitting at a graveside watching flowers turn brown in plastic; counting how many new graves got filled this week, while your grandson makes Christmas paper chains in a classroom. And talks to ghosts.

Is that normal?

Is anything?

The satchel flaps against Ben's school coat like the wings of a baby bird. "It's time, Grandad," he says.

"Time?"

"To let go."

He stretches out one arm, tries to pull the other one free but the old man holds on. "I love you this much, Grandad," he says. Now he pictures the way his daughter used to say the very same thing: *I love you this much.*

I
Love
You
This
Much

He feels the pull, the tug; he feels it everywhere.

The lollipop girl is standing in front of the crossing in bright yellow; candy floss pink hair in wisps around her face; a stud in her nose. She says, "Morning boys." Same thing she says every day.

She thinks about the boy; how he used to come with his mum – a skinny woman in a brown mac; jauntily hung over striped PJs, the bottoms trailing on the pavement. She wore grey slippers; the type that are supposed to go click-clack but instead they went shuffle-shuffle. She's heard the woman has issues, and if she didn't have the lollipop sign in her hands this is when she'd hang commas in the air. His mum has 'issues'. They got worse after his dad was blown up.

Morning boys. Sometimes she winks when she says it; but not the kind of wink she saves only for that fit young window cleaner (proper FIT) who looks like Harry Styles from One Direction. She loves Harry Styles from One Direction. He isn't usually here until after ten, the window cleaner – not Harry Styles from One Direction, more's the pity. She can't talk to him. Sometimes she hangs out at the greasy spoon across the street just to catch a glimpse. It's sad – she knows. SAD in capital letters. It's what she'd write on Facebook if she thought anyone would read it.

One day she'll talk to him.

The old man asked her once if she always wanted to do this.

"Be a lollipop girl?"

No, of course not. She wanted to dance. Go to ballet school. She liked to dream. Kids raised in children's homes are not supposed to dream. She has watched *Billy Elliot* twenty-nine times. She didn't say that.

"Do you need qualifications?"

"I have a certificate."

"In Lollipopping?"

She laughed when he said that. She doesn't laugh very often.

"Yeah," she said. "I have a distinction in Lollipopping."

He laughed. He doesn't laugh very often either. She thought Lollipopping sounded like a dance and she tried to imagine what kind of dance it would be.

"A twirling circles dance," the little boy had said. But she hadn't said it out loud.

She watches the old man now – being tugged along the street. And every few steps the little boy slows, looks back and every time he does she feels something snap. She heard his dad was a soldier; somewhere foreign. She doesn't know what the fighting was about; only that some soldiers don't come home. And the ones who do can be so broken they can't be put back together.

She used to tell people her dad was a soldier, she thought it sounded glamorous – but not now – not anymore. She doesn't know what her dad was.

She thinks about all the broken people; how you can't see the breaks. She wonders if anyone else can hear the sound rain makes when it falls inside your head.

She heard the little boy's mum is in Crickleworth now.

It's a place for broken people. But you don't say that with little commas scratched in the air; you say it with lowered voices, whispers. Like it's a rule no one writes down and she wonders who made that rule; who makes all the rules about what you say and what you don't say. Like kids from children's homes aren't supposed to have dreams; be grateful someone took care of you when your parents didn't. Be grateful for government housing and schemes to get you to work. She thinks if it's someone's job to make the rules they suck at it and it can't be worse than being a nineteen-year-old lollipop girl. She wonders how you apply for a job writing the rules no one says. She thinks the first one she'll write is that everything should happen in dance. Like a scene from a musical. And today's dance will be Lollipopping.

She watches until the boy and the old man turn the corner and wonders what would happen if she wasn't here with her lollipop. If people would pile up by the crossing like they're stuck on one side of the street and they can't get across without her. As if? The world would be just the same only without her in it.

Of course she will be here tomorrow. And the one after that. She'll be here until one day – she won't. Like soldiers who get bombed and no one remembers what they were fighting for. Like the soldier she thinks she sees standing on the crossing – and then she doesn't.

She wraps her fingers over the pole of her lollipop and thinks how she'd like to pirouette herself all the way home.

She wonders if anyone'll notice if she isn't here tomorrow.

Definitely not the one who looks like Harry Styles.

I will she hears. But no one's there.

The teacher stands with her hands pressed against a cold

radiator, eyes fixed on the playground where the first of the children say goodbye to parents at the gate.
    And soon… they'll skip.
    Into.
    Her.
    Classroom.
    And.
    For.
    The rest of the day.
    All her thoughts.
    And words.
    Will be.
    Interrupted.
    The bell will ring in seven minutes.

On the table, in a wooden box are sheets of coloured paper, white glue in little pots with plastic red nozzles. Safe glue; *odourless, non-toxic, won't stick your fingers together Health and Safety approv*ed glue. By next week the paper chains will have opened up and fluttered to the floor like giant pieces of confetti. But she hopes they'll last at least until.
    Wednesday.
    After Wednesday all the classrooms will be empty and she'll be drinking mulled wine in an empty living room while the lights threaded haphazardly on a small *seen-better-days* Christmas tree blink on and off. On and off. On and.
    Off.
    And where all her thoughts will flow without interruption but if you listen you might just hear her heart break a little more – it will make a small sound. A soft rustle of a sound; a lot like paper chains ungluing in a silent classroom that.

No one.
Will.
Ever.
Hear.

It's been a year since he left.

She's not even told her mum. He took it all; everything he owned like a Pharaoh preparing for the afterlife; an afterlife that did not include her but the blonde bimbo he met at the gym and who he helped celebrate reaching her thirty inches off *all over* with a whole different kind of.

Workout.

He bundled himself book by book, jumper by jumper, box by box into his VW Beetle and drove away, leaving her standing on the pavement with her hand bent into an almost wave and wondering what happens next.

She thought she might move, might give up teaching all together. Might buy a new Christmas tree. But she won't. She'll pretend he's still there until she can't pretend.

Noises lift off the playground: excited chitter chatter of Christmas in children's voices. She thinks about gluing paper chains with white *odourless, non-toxic, won't stick your fingers together Health and Safety approved* glue. Chains that will come undone.

And she thinks, in these *before it starts* moments; before the children come in and arrange their coloured pens and their pencils in neat lines and stare at the front with expectant faces, that today will be better.

Today the radiator might actually come on.

Today when she gets home he might be sat waiting for her. His VW Beetle with its books and its jumpers and its boxes will be parked outside number seven and he'll say how sorry he is, he made a mistake. It didn't work out with the girl at the gym. Then he'll ask to come in.

As her breath coats the window and her fingers dance out the shapes of snowflakes she sees old Albert Clarke standing at the gate with Ben and she sees the boy lean in and slowly plant a kiss on his grandad's cheek. She wonders if the boy's mum will be home in time for Christmas. She thinks about what happened to his dad, and what kind of Christmas they'll have now. She hates all the news stories about war. Wars are everywhere, but it's what's played out on the inside that people never see that hurt the most; inside heads, inside homes; inside schools.

Two years ago, at Christmas, something terrible happened in a school in America. She wonders if they got as far as making paper chains.

Last week she thought she saw a man in a uniform standing at the gate staring at her classroom. In America a young boy walked into a classroom and.

BANG.

She wonders what happens to all the bad sounds. She'd like to put them in a box and bury them too deep to hear. Twenty-seven died in that school in America. Not just children.

She hopes the happy Christmas sounds will drown out everything else; like paper chains opening up because *odourless, non-toxic, won't stick your fingers together Health and Safety approved* glue doesn't keep all the pieces together and sooner or later everything comes.

Undone.

But not today.

Today they will make Christmas paper chains in red and green. She has found some gold paper; just for Ben. He says it's a happy colour. And he told her she needed a happy colour. He said angels have golden wings. And his hand had slipped into hers. He told her you can feel colour with your fingers. And then he'd whispered *you deserve better.* He'd whispered it so softly she wasn't sure she'd even heard it.

As the bell goes and the children come in, she holds a piece of gold paper between her fingers and she hopes the little boy was right. She thinks if there is a VW Beetle parked outside number seven maybe.

Just.
Maybe.
She won't.
Let him come in.

Albert Clarke sits in the cemetery; folds old fingers around a dried up rose while the words of a nursery rhyme repeat in his head: *they couldn't put Humpty together again.* He thinks about Ben's father. He walked out of the blast with everything intact. A miracle they said.

But they couldn't see what was on the inside.

You can hear it rattling he used to tell Susan. And she would say yes, she could hear it too and he'd watch her press her head to his and for a while it was like they connected to something no one else could.

He was hailed the miracle soldier; the one who survived when no one else did. Who got to come home to his wife and his son and everything was supposed to be normal. And the only one who seemed to notice was a six-year-old boy who asked his grandad why Daddy was already a ghost.

His daughter forgot to take her medication.
Her husband forgot how to be the person he used to be.
And one day he was gone.
BANG.

She was in the hospital saying there was a soldier sat at her bedside while a doctor wrote *hallucinations* on a chart. And Ben was standing in their empty house saying *Daddy's with Nana now*.

He lowers himself onto aching knees, presses his hands around what's left of the rose and mumbles a prayer.

It's a small moment, a fleeting, transient, *did it really happen?* moment and it's over in a held-breath but he knows he was here. He knows it from the uprush of warm air on the back of his hand. He has felt his son-in-law before. He has never felt Gertie. But he has felt *him* and he knows why.

I'm sorry.

"I know, Son," he says. "I do know."

People say only cowards take their own life. But they're wrong. So very wrong.

Albert doesn't know how long he's been there but he feels the ache everywhere. He thinks about Ben in school. Wonders if he's made his paper chains. He thinks about Susan. And the thing he knows he has to do. Finally. He must pay her a visit. He must tell her she *did* see her husband at her bedside, he *was* there.

Old lips fold around the shape of the *should've been saids* and the *too hard to says* and the *have to be saids*. He has to say it now – he has to say it before they all fall down.

I forgive you.

As he whispers it, he is sure someone touches his hand.

Paper chains: reds and greens and golds in a silent classroom.

A teacher stands at the misted window and draws circles with a finger. Ben is the last to leave. He is at the gate, shuffling his feet in an almost dance as he waits for his grandad; satchel flapping. The old man is late. He is never late. She should call the boy back inside but—

It happens right before she sees the old man turn the corner. Right before she hears the rustle of a paper chain – when there is no breeze.

It is a day for strange things. These are the words she will write later in her diary, with her revised list of Christmas plans.

And resolutions.

First one: call Mother.

She will write how she saw a little boy hugging a man dressed as a soldier at the school gate but when she blinked he was gone.

She will write how she decided to walk home and saw the lollipop girl, with the pink hair and the stud in her nose, twirling circles and dancing herself along the high street with a man who looks an awful lot like Harry Styles from One Direction.

And she will write how when she saw the old man and she is sure there was a gentle hippedy hop in those old legs.

And when everyone else has gone – after Wednesday, when the school is shut for the holidays, she will think again about the soldier at the gate saying goodbye to his son. And how it's in the moments that most don't see, in *the glimpses, and the glances and the not quite sure it even happens* – when life changes the most.

We all fall down she will tell herself; and we must all get back up. A little boy taught her that. She has a feeling she won't see the soldier again.

And in an empty classroom over the Christmas holidays, golden paper chains will open like angels' wings and fall quietly down.

About this story
Placed Second in Leicester Short Story Prize, 2018, published in *Leicester Writes Anthology, Volume 2*, June 2018. I am particularly excited about this as one of the judges was my favourite short story writer, Jon McGregor.

Jigsaw

I'm not like other kids. Mum says it all the time when she thinks I'm not listening. She says it isn't normal for people to disappear.

But for me it is.

It's a chronological disorder. They call it lots of different things. Gran calls it *The Gift*. I catch her looking at me sometimes like she thinks if she stares long enough something will happen. Perhaps she thinks I'll become pixelated like when the satellite TV goes weird and that I'll vanish. But it doesn't work that way. I never totally disappear.

Sometimes they call it 'episodes' and sometimes they call it 'spells' but wizards make spells which means something magic and enchanted and it isn't like that. I call it travelling.

I don't know when it's going to happen and I can't control it. It starts with the smell of burning which is weird, given what happened, and it feels like I'm gone for hours but really it's only seconds. I suppose it's a bit like finding a land at the back of the wardrobe.

My name is Leonardo Renoir Hope and I am a seven-year-old traveller. Hope means 'to long for.' The thing I long for is to finish the jigsaw I started with my dad that day. He said, "We'll finish it tomorrow." But sometimes tomorrow doesn't come.

Did you know that there are 60,000 fires in the home every year in Britain and that more than 700 people die?

I keep a book under my pillow. I call it 'Our Book of Facts.' It was my dad's idea. He said I should write down about my travels. He said details are really important and writing it down is a way of remembering. I try to remember my dad's hands, the way they looked when they turned the pages. I imagine my hand fitting into his, like pulling on a warm glove.

And then I think: what if I forget?

I've got to find him. I've got to put things right.

My dad said that the world is about rules. He said there are rules for everything. With jigsaws he always started with the corners. So in a special section of our book, after the bit I call 'My Dictionary,' for all my new words, are 'The Rules.' They are the rules we were trying to figure out about travelling.

I haven't seen Dad since that day but I know he is somewhere because everyone is somewhere.

I saw Grandad after he died. He died in Bognor Regis but he was born in Germany. He was struck by lightning when he was trying to fix the satellite dish.

Rule Number 1: Nothing totally disappears.

So I've been trying to find Dad. I've been thinking if we'd finished the jigsaw would there still have been a fire? That's when I got the idea that if I could change one thing maybe Dad would still be here. But that means I have to figure out what really happened.

I used to think that everybody travels, but they don't. Dad said only special people travel. But if that's true then why didn't he travel? And then sometimes I think maybe he *did* travel, but he's lost his RADAR (which stands for RAdio Detection And Range). If RADAR is made up of radio waves that can bounce off raindrops and travel in space, then why can't it work in heaven?

Did you know the first jigsaw puzzle was made to teach children geography?

I wonder if there's a map of heaven? I wonder if it has streets and a house like ours. I wonder if my dad is waiting there for us.

I know about parallel universes, I just don't know how you get to heaven.

But I know the one place that I will find my dad.

Rule Number 2: You can only travel backwards.

I saw a film once when a man kept re-living the same day over and over again. I think it was so he could get it right, so he could make it perfect. That's what's happening to me. I keep travelling back to that day; to that Saturday. Finishing the jigsaw is my way of making it perfect.

Rule number 3: If you think too much about a time you get stuck there.

Did you know that most fires happen at night when people are sleeping?

Dad knew about fire. Dad knew about a lot of things. He knew about 'flashovers' too. A flashover is 'when everything bursts into flames.' I don't know why my dad went back into our house that day. That's one of the things I'm trying to figure out.

It was Dad who told me: "Once you have the corners, you can make the edges."

When I'm going to travel and I smell the burning I think about Dad. I try to remember his face; the way it creased up when he was making a joke and the way he threw his head back when he found something really funny. I press the memory into the air so hard I think I can see it hanging there like when you stare at a light bulb for too long.

Sometimes I think I might run out of tears. I never do.

My sister is only four and she's called Monet; Monet Hope with no middle name. I think my mum ran out of artists' names when she called the rabbits Rembrandt and Picasso. I look at Monet sometimes and I think if anyone's going to forget Dad, it's her.

Mum stayed in her bedroom for a long time after that

day. She kept the curtains closed. I think maybe that's *her* way of disappearing. If Dad was here he would know what to do. He would know how to reach her.

But that's just it.

My dad's the one who's dead but it's like my mum is the one who stopped living.

The words next to Mum in my dictionary used to be 'pretty' and 'kind' and 'my best friend' (apart from Dad) but I crossed it out and now it says 'sad.' I was going to write in capital letters 'SAD', like that, but that means it's a shout and she never shouts that she's sad – she just is.

I'm like my mum.

I never tell her how my heart feels like it's got a crack down the middle and that every time I cry I think it's going to break apart. People sing songs about 'broken hearts.' I used to think, "That's silly, hearts can't break."

But they can.

After Grandad died Gran came to live with us. She said she loved Grandad. I asked her what 'love' means. She said, "This," and she hugged me. Then she said, "Love feels like coming home."

Mum blames Gran for what happened but it was an accident. That means 'something that happens by chance.' She forgot to turn off the gas after she made cocoa and left a tea towel too close to the flames. That's because she's very old and she forgets things. Mum said the word for it is 'senile.'

But next to the word Gran in my dictionary I didn't write senile. I wrote 'sorry.' And I wrote 'funny' and 'used to be young.' That's because one word can mean lots of things.

My grandad used to be young. He was a soldier. I saw him a lot when I first started to travel. I told him who I was and he told me lots of things – that's when Dad said I should write them down.

Did you know there were 400,000 German soldiers in Britain after the Second World War?

Grandad said, "Tell me what's going to happen in the future." He spoke in a funny accent. He clicked his letters as he spoke. I didn't answer him.

Rule Number 4: You mustn't tell.

So I asked Grandad to tell me about Gran. He said he loved her on the day he met her. When I asked *him* what love means he said, "It's a warm feeling that starts in your toes and spreads all the way up to your smile."

I saw Dad when he was young too. I saw him twice. The first time was at The Tate Gallery in London. He was supposed to meet a girl there but she never showed up. I watched him on the steps. Then he asked another girl what time it was. When she turned around I thought my heart would burst through my chest. It was my mum.

Later I asked Dad if I would still be here if the other girl had shown up. I asked him what would have happened if he hadn't met my mum and fallen in love with her. Then I asked *him* what love means. He looked at me for ages, the way he did sometimes when he was really thinking hard about something. I saw his eyes fill up like he was going to cry but he didn't.

Then he said, "When you love someone, Leo, you can't imagine life without them."

"No," I said.

Then he smirked. "The other girl was a scientist. If she was your mum you might be called Einstein or Galileo!"

Then he threw back his head and laughed. I copied him and we laughed so hard we thought we were going to die from it.

When I saw Grandad after he died I hugged him but I think I did it too hard and for too long because there was something odd about his face when he looked back at me. Maybe you can tell people things without telling them? He gave me a photograph and I watched him scribble a message on the back. It was written in German. It said 'Vergissmeinnicht.' That means *Forget me not.* I took the photograph back to Gran.

When I asked her about the message she said it's what Grandad said to her on the day they met. Then she cried.

Rule Number 5: It's better not to take things back with you.

There were lots of things that got burned in the fire. I heard Mum talk about insurance. That means 'money that's used to replace things.' But she said there are some things you can't replace. I wonder if she meant Dad. But I still couldn't find him. I *did* find the letters that Dad wrote to Mum when they were at college; ones that talked about love.

Mum said love means "To need someone so much it hurts." I didn't want Mum to hurt. That's why I took the letters for her to find.

Violation Rule Number 5.

Dad said, "Sometimes it's okay to break the rules if it's for the right reason." And I figured that if the reason was to put things right then that was the right reason.
But it just made Mum more sad (SAD).

Rule Number 5 (amended): NEVER take things back.

The other time I saw Dad he was ten years old. He looked at me for a long time. Then he said, "Don't I know you?"
"You will in the future."

Later I asked Dad about it and he said he never forgot. It's like that with little kids. They always believe.

When they rebuilt our house and painted the living room green, when it should have been magnolia, they found a piece of the jigsaw. The one we never got to finish. The edge was scorched. I tucked it inside the 'Our Book of Facts'. It's like I have a part of him with me. I never told Mum. She doesn't believe. She said she does but I know she thinks that Dad is gone. She says it all the time. I wonder if she remembers his face.

I'd collected lots of facts from that day but I still couldn't figure out what really happened. It's like I had all the pieces spread out on the table but they weren't in the right order.

Dad said, "Once you have all the edges you need to fill in the pieces from the outside."

Dad forgot to put the batteries back into the smoke detector after we burnt toast when Mum was out that time. The alarm kept bleeping for ages even though we waved a tea towel in front of it and stomped our feet like those gay men doing the River Dance. Gay means 'cheerful.' Gran says that Graham Norton off the TV is very cheerful. She likes Graham Norton. He was on TV the day that Grandad got struck by lightning.

Sometimes I lose Dad's face. It breaks up into pixels. That's how I know that time is running out. That's how I knew I had to find a way to travel more; to find the other pieces. So I had this idea…

I did it at night. I tried it with torches at first like the one Mum uses to look inside the smoke detectors that are on the ceiling to see if the batteries haven't leaked. I flashed it really fast right into my eyes. I did it for fifteen minutes. It didn't make me travel but it made me see swirly things in the air and feel like I was going to throw up.

Cool.

So then I decided to switch on the lights in my bedroom really fast: click on, click off, click on, click off, on, off, on, off...

It worked! It *really* worked! The lights would blur into one and then I would smell the burning. The more I did it the more exhausted I was but it didn't matter. I had to do it.

And even though I still couldn't find Dad I had to start changing things before *he* disappeared.

I decided to put the batteries back in the smoke detector and then when the fire came we would know. But I couldn't reach the smoke detector and I couldn't get back to the day we burned the toast and acted cheerful like Graham Norton to remind Dad to put the batteries back in. That's because, as I said, I was stuck on the day of the fire.

I thought that maybe I could hide the cocoa but Gran would probably have hot milk anyway which means she would still turn on the gas.

And that's when I knew there was only one way: I would have to tell.

Violation Rule Number 4.

But there was one thing for certain: I absolutely positively MUST NEVER tell ME.

Rule Number 6: NEVER RUN INTO YOURSELF (and that *is* in capital letters because *it is* a shout).

But the thing is... I did.

I had it all figured out, I was going to tell Gran. It would probably make her scream but it didn't matter; she's senile anyway. I would tell her there was going to be a fire and that she mustn't make cocoa. I would say that she had to tell Dad, "DON'T go back in the house." I would write in her hand if I had to.

Then I thought, since Gran forgets things, it would be better to write a letter to Dad that explained everything. But the thing is: THE thing is... I was forgetting about the final rule, the one we were still working on.

Rule Number 7: You CAN'T change things.

Maybe that's why I never travelled for long enough to do any of those things. I never saw Gran, not even long enough to make her scream. I never got to say, "Don't go back in the house, Dad," the way I did over and over into my pillow at night.

I don't know how many times I had to travel by flicking the lights on and off and thinking about Dad before I could finally make out the picture. But I did, in the end...

It was Dad's voice that woke me up that night. I forced my eyes to open but the lids felt heavy, and my eyes were rolling around, slipping to the bottom.

I heard Dad's voice again.

But this time I knew what he was saying. He said, "FIRE!" When I opened my eyes this time they stayed open.

"Get up, Leo," he said and I felt his hands on my shoulders. "Get up!"

The first thing I felt was the heat. It was like when you open the oven door and the heat gushes out onto your face and Mum screams out and says, "Don't stand too close!"

But it was too late.

Dad looked like a ghost, there was a huge blanket over his head and he said, "Come on."

I stumbled towards the doorway wondering for a moment if it was terrible nightmare. I squeezed the skin of my arm; pinched it really hard.

But I wasn't dreaming.

When I reached the landing I saw my mum and she was holding onto my sister carefully climbing down the stairs. At each step Mum was feeling the way with her foot and I realised I was holding my breath as I watched them.

There was thick smoke like someone's hand was smothering my face and there was a cracking sound. Maybe that was the sound my heart made when it broke in the middle. Bits of black floated in the air like flapping birds. I felt my hand slide into Dad's and he yanked me forwards. I closed my eyes and willed the world to disappear.

Dad was holding onto me, urging me to follow my mum and my sister down the stairs where the wood was all melted and twisted like the jigsaw on the table in the living room.

Then there was a terrible tearing sound and I felt Dad's hand wrenched out of mine, snapped away from me. I tried to scream but the words got sucked away in the roar. Huge orange flames came up between us. Dad was trapped upstairs. Mum was shouting something from the hallway. I looked back.

"DAD!"

"Keep going, Leo!" he said. "Keep going!"

"But, Dad?"

"I'll climb down the drainpipe... it'll be okay Leo. I promise. Don't look back..."

That's the last thing he said to me. "Don't look back."

So I didn't look back. I didn't. And all the time I was thinking, "Dad will climb down the drainpipe and it will all be okay because he promised." I pressed the words into the hot smoky air until they stuck.

I held my breath and jumped the last three steps losing my footing and it was like the ground came up and hit my knees. My throat burned, my eyes streamed like I was crying but I wasn't.

Not yet.

I felt my belly brushing against the floor as I scrambled on my elbows.

I kept thinking, where's Dad?

Then I saw it.

I saw the gap where the light came through the front door and I knew I was going to get out safely. It was going to be okay.

Or it should have been.

The thing is I couldn't have known it was going to happen because the warning wouldn't have worked.

There was a piece missing, the one that would show me why Dad went back into the house. Maybe it was the piece that got left behind in the box or maybe it was the piece I had all along. But without it I would never see. And that meant I couldn't finish the jigsaw.

I still had to travel one more time. And that time I did see.

I was standing by the table watching as the jigsaw pieces bubbled and melted from the corners inwards until there was nothing left. That's when I finally saw. Dad had made it down the drainpipe and was looking at me. I wanted to shout, "Go back outside! GO back outside, Dad!" Except the words wouldn't come, like when you're having a nightmare, pushing out silent air. Dad was holding something in his arms. My lips fell open. I lifted my hands to cover my eyes because I didn't want to see. Because the thing in Dad's arms was me. It was the first time I saw what I look like when I travel.

Violation Rule Number 6.

That was the moment that time split like an atom.
Flashover.
Silence.
No one ever survives a flashover. And that means I must have died too.

I open my eyes. There's something rolling between my fingers. I'm in our living room only now it's painted magnolia and not green anymore. The air is cool on my face.

I hear my name being called. I turn around. It's Dad. Oh God, it's Dad! It's Dad! I want to stare at every part of his face, to take it in because I don't know if it's real. I see Monet. She's on the couch and she's staring at me and Mum is reading an art book. I haven't seen her do that since that day.

Dad speaks again. "Well don't you want to finish the puzzle?"

I look at the table with the jigsaw that isn't melted or twisted anymore. I look at Dad's hands.

"What day is it?" I say and Dad looks at me kind of funny.

"Sunday," he says.

It's like that film with the man who wakes up and there's a different song on the radio. It's not Saturday anymore! A scream catches in my throat. I look around the room. But something's wrong. I say, "Where's Gran?"

This time they all turn to look at me like I'm crazy and I think for a second I am.

"At home with Grandad I should think," says Mum and I watch her eyebrows climb into peaks.

"In Bognor?" I say and she lays the book down on her knee and looks at me.

"Where else?" she says.

"He didn't get struck by lightning in Bognor Regis?"

I feel Dad's eyes burning the bit of skin at the back of my neck.

I hear my sister laugh. I look at Dad. He stares for a moment like he's thinking hard, then he throws his head back and laughs. I do too. That's when I finally let go.

"What's up with you!" says Mum shaking her head.

So then I realise.

Rule Number 7 (amended): You CAN change things.

And I turn to Dad. "You can change things," I say. "You *can* change things. YOU CAN!"

It happened before the flashover; when I was in my Dad's arms. If I was travelling that meant I had to be somewhere else.

I was in Germany and it was a very long time ago. I was standing in front of a little boy.

"I have to tell you something," I said. "But without *really* telling you." I was talking in English but the words came out in German.

Very cool.

I said, "NEVER get satellite." Then I realised he didn't know what satellite was, but he would. "And don't let Gran watch Graham Norton."

He looked at me like I was a total Freak, with a capital F.

Then I remembered something else. "Vergissmeinnicht," I said.

Then I disappeared.

I look at Mum who's still reading and at Monet who's still staring at me but now she's smiling.

I think, "You don't need RADAR to find your way back because heaven is anywhere you want it to be."

I look down at my open hand where a piece of jigsaw sits. I scrutinise the edge for a scorch mark and at first I think I can still see it, but then I think I can't.

Our hands touch, me and my dad as we press the last piece into the puzzle. He smiles at me.

My book is open on the table at the dictionary part. Next to the word 'love' I've written 'Dad'.

About this story
Published in *Making Changes,* Bridge House Publishing, 2008. This is the first short story that was ever accepted for publication and it came from waking up one morning with just the opening line: *I'm not like other kids, Mum says it all the time when she thinks I'm not listening. She says it isn't normal for people to disappear...* I had no idea where it was going so I let it happen... 'as if like magic'. That's what I love so much about writing. I am probably more proud of this little story than any other because it marked the beginning of my publishing journey. It is a story that is open to interpretation. I think story resolutions need to feel satisfactory but they also need to leave some ambiguity for the reader to make up their own mind. What do you think *really* happened? I had to put this one in and give it another lease of life since it was first published over ten years ago.

Goldfish Parade

Round and round you go.
A stumbling, traipsing, fumbling of wearied footsteps.
Not a parade – more a shuffle. A shuffle of broken feet trying to march, trying to still be soldiers.
A stumble breaks the circle, the ground rises up with a slap and a groan. Hard on fragile bones.
Get up! You have to get up. And you have to keep on getting up. Because one day, one glorious day, all of this will be a memory. What they'll never tell you is how it will always be a fight to get up.
But for now... round and round you go.
Like goldfish on parade – but these goldfish will never forget.

2019 – Blog post titled: **Countdown**

The writer stares at the flashing cursor; ring finger poised, hovering, wondering if words are enough.

Last night words were mumbled into pink cotton – in case he heard, stirred in his sleep, realised she really is weird.

Aren't all writers weird?

He has nothing to fear. It's just a story. She likes to talk to it.

Who does that, babe?

Me. I do that.

Even imagined conversations are probably weird.

It's part of her charm, he loves her anyway. In three days 'I do' will mean forever.

It will be a horror story, not the *I do* part; the *story* story.

She must get inside it, climb inside the heads of her characters. Talk to them.

What was it really like to be a prisoner?
Like goldfish on parade. Round and round we go.

Blog Post: **Be Prepared**

The writer blogs about a honeymoon, not yet booked: she wants to change her passport first. She talks about life, feeling blessed, second chances. It's meant to be about writing and so she writes: always prepare, do your research first. She waffles, posts, edits, edits some more and reposts. Someone likes it immediately.

Then she writes.

Not her blog but the story – *the* story. The part that comes after her prologue and her fancy title. It's the story she has always promised herself she'd write.

> *Elsie runs her fingers along imaginary lace, delighting in the giddiness of the moment. In two days Alfred will slide gold onto her finger and change her identity. Not just a new name but a new role. The youngest of thirteen and now it's her turn. A new life to build and rooms to fill. She feels for the smooth fabric and stares at the simple but beautiful elegance of the dress, understated, like her. Someone once told her the worlds we imagine really can become, and this time the New Year, 1934, will start with a new Elsie. But right now in her parents' house in her small box room this moment cannot be contained by the floral print wallpaper. This tiny moment will pass, unnoticed, just as she read about the Nazis in Germany a month or so ago and she'd asked, what are Nazis, Alf?*
>
> *Nothing to worry about he'd whispered, my sweet Elsie. Nothing to worry about.*
>
> *It was in the paper she said.*

Tomorrows chip wrappings, he said fumbling with a newspaper from two days ago, something about a new motor company in Japan: how is that news? None of it means anything to them in Blighty...

Blog Post: **Gut Feelings**

The writer blogs what she feels and how feelings go deep, and she connects it to a piece on deep character viewpoint. She says how excitement lives in the same hollow place as fear and anxiety and it's about knowing the difference. But *this, this* is excitement. She feels it like a bubble rising to the surface of a champagne glass... he loves her, no doubts, no regrets, no fear. Last time she got this close there wasn't even a ring, just a desperate ache. Last time is a world built from broken dreams. Broken dreams and almosts. Broken dreams and almosts and... cancer.

She has written many stories about that.

Scribbles, doodles, notes that Elsie folds into the pages of a journal she keeps shut in a bedroom drawer. She fears everything and nothing all at the same time. That he will take it all back and say he made a mistake; he'd rather marry Maud from no. 16. Or—

Or nothing.

Alfred loves her.

Some things you can be sure about – and she is sure about that. She glances at the engagement ring, a simple diamond for a simple, honest and open-minded man; a man who loves her and he'd laugh if she said maybe he likes Maud from no. 16. She loves the way Alfred laughs. It was the first thing she noticed.

Blog post: **10 Reasons Why**

It is inspired by a Netflix show of a similar name, but not the same – not at all the same. She asked him last night: tell me why you love me? Tell me ten reasons why...

She said the words as he zipped his suit onto a hanger inside a black Moss Bros bag and she made sure the waistcoat, the burgundy tie and handkerchief were there, and he had his shoes. His 'expensive' shoes. Her 'expensive' dress is zipped into a white bag at her mum's. His best man arrives soon to take him... and then tomorrow... a date engraved inside a ring, so he can never forget. As if.

You know why I love you he said, stop fishing.

Fishing? Tell me.

I'm trying to get ready; you said you'd kill me if I forgot anything.

Yeah. And I will.

He finished and didn't say anything else at first, then he looked at her as she stood in the doorway with that wonderful smile of his – that he says is because of her – and she felt the heat seep through from that Pooh mug of hers that she clasped with both hands and he said, Your mind. He shoved a toiletry bag into his rucksack and before she could say yeah and she'd done all that work at the gym on her glutes and he loved her mind first, he added, you have a wonderful smile that lights up everything. So, that too. And your spirit... your optimism – it's infectious... your love... how many is that?

But they didn't get to finish because a knock kick-started the dog into bark mode and they realised it was time for him to go.

People love a winter wedding.

Alfred said they had to choose a date quickly

since the British Army needed him. Don't worry, it won't be yet, no Elsie, not yet, but I want to make an honest woman of you anyway.

Everything about us is honest she whispers.

And she makes a wish as she kisses him goodnight, she won't see him now – it's unlucky to see him before the wedding. She whispers her wish into his thick grey overcoat as they embrace: how she needs him more than the British Army – that they will have some time together first... she asks God and later she'll write it in her journal because writing the words keeps them safe.

Blog post: **Today is my new favourite day**

The writer has borrowed the words from her literary hero, Pooh, and from her brother and his wife who had it inscribed in their wedding rings when they were married last year. Then she posts one word: Yay! And that is all. The post is written before the girls are up to remind her this is the day and how does she feel? She feels calm. She flicks bubbles between her toes as she bathes by pink scented tealight and reminds herself that this is the last time she will do this as a single woman. It's a moment tinted with rosy edges, but it's real. It has never felt more real. Candles remind her of the ones not here and she has a candle that will burn today on the altar, by the Christmas tree – still there in mid-January to guide the wise men home. Her candle is for those whose light lit the way to this moment: their grandparents, his dad, *him* until the cancer broke everything. And she knows God is still there because of this second chance. Not second best, never that: second chances are better. Sinatra said something about that. It's lovelier. And it is.

They did it. Alfred all handsome and blue eyes, salty tears on cheeks and blushes as they kissed. It was perfect. Not big, not lavish but perfect because it was them, so them and when he held her hand and lead her out to the peal of wedding bells she knew. He was hers forever. The winter sun reflected in her wedding band. It lit up the path ahead that no one could put asunder.

Blog post: **We did it!**

No profound title or writerly message just some clichéd ramblings about new chapters, clean pages and hope. Three days ago she made her promise to a man who looked at her as if she was his everything – as he is to her – and she talked of what she calls a 'minimoon': three days spent with American friends in London and how her feet still have not hit the ground. Perfect in every way. It sounds so clichéd; so *obvious*; it's what people say but it is obvious. Love is real. Words she imagines graffitied on the sea wall or etched deep into skin.

Maybe marriage is like floating through life she writes and someone says that's the wedding, marriage is the bumpy landing.

She pictures two sets of feet side by side facing the world no matter what it brings; no matter how 'bumpy' the road. They have ridden out many storms. *Okay alone, stronger together.* It's their motto. They both know this. She also knows it sounds corny, some might say idealistic, but THEY haven't been through what she has; what he has. THEY don't know.

If you believe; truly believe – then – the bubbles never break.

Next week they go back to work.

There is no honeymoon; just three days of togetherness and making plans during brisk walks in winter sunshine. They have it all... until—
...the cloud sweeps in and whips their hands apart. Elsie wonders if God has stopped listening; if she should have shouted not whispered. She still feels the warmth of his hand in hers long after he's set sail from Southampton.
"Be safe, Alfred," she says. "Come back soon."
"I will, Elsie, love. I will." It's what she still hears as she stands and the wind flaps washing on her mother's line and she wonders how she will fill the time now. They should have been looking for a home to call theirs.

Blog post: **Life with a new name**

Why – the writer blogs – do people ask her what married life is like? She tells them it's like her co-habiting life but with a new name; like a story with a new title and then she blogs about the importance of story titles. She leaves the post half-written and wanders into the other room with her china 'Mrs' mug, one half of a pair and yet still whole, still the same... *okay alone, stronger together. Greater than the sum of two parts.*

Someone once told her how a union between two people has to make something greater than each of them. She doesn't remember who said it, it's very LA – probably one of their American friends.

They have not finished opening the cards or the gifts and the living room is filled up with silvery white bags and wilting helium balloons; and cards – but there will never be enough space for them all. They have to stand up in batches like a relay: each appointed a day before being placed lovingly into a keepsake box. She doesn't want to think about a day, she hopes many years from now, when one of them will be looking at this alone. What will they remember about the day? That it was truly perfect.

Winter weddings *are* the best she mumbles.

Her heart is filled up; it's all so overwhelming she just sits with her feet on the warm wooden floors, perched on the edge of the leather couch sipping lukewarm coffee from her Mrs mug – staring. Eyes shift to the band on her finger and she dares to dream of what it means and how if she could go back in time what would her younger self think if she said she would be fifty before she married? She thinks about a blog post she wrote about that – not being fifty – but what you would say if you met your younger self. What advice she would give. *Don't worry so much. You are stronger than you ever thought you were. It's okay to be alone... but don't be afraid to love again.*

What would you do differently? she asked him last night. If you could go back.

Nothing he said. He didn't even need time to think about it. She had been almost asleep when the light flashed on momentarily, then the bed sank in and his ice cold feet were digging into hers.

What about the *bad* stuff, though? You'd go through it all again?

It makes us who we are he said.

And she had thought about that.

She had thought about that a lot.

How even in her years of grief she knew she had reached a point when she would not go back, even if she could; when she liked the lessons she'd learned – the person she'd become – only of course if she could bring him back from the dead she would – but – that could never happen. It only happens in fiction. She thinks about Elsie.

She read a novel once about a woman in the First World War. Her husband was missing in action. After seven years she remarried and then he came home. What a dilemma, could you have them both? How could you choose? She guesses it must've really happened to someone. She is thankful not to have that dilemma.

She wonders if she had to reach that point, that final acceptance, before she could truly move on. Because when she did, he came along. Now her husband – and now she has her answer – she would never go back. She is still getting used to saying *this is my husband. My husband thinks, hubby said...*

Yes.

Yes what? he'd said as he pulled her closer, into a spoon.

Yes you're right. We need to go through it to be who we are. It shapes us.

His hand reached for hers and squeezed softly under the butterfly duvet.

I like who we are, we're different, but we work.

Yes he said. We do.

A tighter squeeze.

Never let go: words she whispers silently. *Can't lose you.*

Do you think it was the same for Alfred and Elsie?

Who's Alfred and Elsie?

No one. Go to sleep.

A letter arrives and she stares, focuses on the slant of the small familiar handwriting: and the first thing Elsie does is lift it to her face, seeking his scent. She worries she has forgotten and her mind convinces her she can smell him between the words: soap and tobacco. She wonders if he does the same. It takes too long for letters to arrive. She writes how she dreams of their own home; imagines it as she walks home with her sister from Cooke's Jellied Eel and Mash Shop after the afternoon shift.

He writes how he misses her, and he has asked about leave again. He hopes to be home in the summer. She looks out of her mother's kitchen and feels the soap bubbles break as she looks at the sky and thinks summer is a place as far away as him. He says Bermuda is beautiful and that she ought to see it and maybe one day she will...

It's not right her mother tells her, for a husband to be away so soon. How can you get to know one another if—

He has his duty her dad says. It's what he has to do. They have a lifetime together.

Yes she whispers. We have forever.

Blog post: **Lost**

The writer says small words make good writing prompts.

'Lost' is one of those words because it can mean something tangible that you can hold in your hand, or something like a thought, a memory... a moment. And, as she knows, it can mean a person. She has been married for a few weeks when she writes this, but Elsie is still waiting for Alfred a year after they wed. With stories you can play with time, a year is gone in one line of narrative. Two in a heartbeat, three in a blink. Four in a? And as she writes she thinks how time is one of those things that can be lost.

I want to make everything count she tells him later as she rests her head on his chest and listens to the soft *lub-dup* of his heartbeat. We know what can happen; *she* knows what can happen when love is lost.

You never really lose a person he tells her. It's energy: changing form.

She likes that; how did he get to be so wise?

He takes her hand.

She likes how he holds her hand whenever they're out and shows the world she is part of him and he is part of her. She remembers how once even that one simple gesture felt so strange, like she had to learn to love again, to let go of what happened. She knew when you love you can lose, but it is no life if it is built on the fear of loss, now is it? Like Elsie she thinks. Did she let go of the fear? Hold onto the energy?

It *is* all about the energy; about how it fuses... *okay alone, stronger together*... and she thinks how she will blog about that tomorrow: it's the first law of thermodynamics.

Is that what happens when someone dies, is that what happens to the energy? It moves into the next person; the one holding their hand? And if they are not together when it happens, then where does it go?

Later as he climbs into bed she has forgotten what she said she would blog about tomorrow. She's thinking about Elsie.

I love you.

I love you more, babe.

I will always love you.

Ditto.

Time loses meaning. These are the words Elsie scribbles into her journal and wonders if this time Alfred's leave won't be cancelled. He sounds upbeat, like it's just a thing but once he comes home they will have more time than they know what to do with. She trails her hand over her belly and imagines the baby they might have had by now.

Two years pass in a beat. Three in a blink. Four... and still no leave. She hears that word again: Nazi and she hears her dad talking about it in whispers, about events in Germany, but she pushes it aside. Just words.

I love you, Alf.
Love you more.

Blog post: **Character Roles**

'The writer' is how she identifies herself. And 'Mother' – to fur babies (two cats, one dog). She thinks about human babies she might have had, had things been different. Like Elsie. The writer is too old for babies; she mourned for the 'almost' babies long ago. But she is a mother. Her stories are her babies too. She has had three stories accepted already this year. She still writes as her single name, as if wife and writer are two different people. Two sides of the same lucky sixpence – like the one she wore taped inside her shoe on her wedding day.

He says they need to book their honeymoon; he says it when the passport finally arrives in her new name and she smiles. Yes. She stares at the picture (about fifteen attempts on his phone: against the blank wall in the lounge: no shadow, don't smile, hair away from face). No says the computer: try again. Try again. Try again. Until finally – yes! Now she studies the shape of her nose, her eyes. She looks more like a villain; she thinks the States will refuse her entry based on looking like a convict.

He laughs when she says that. You crack me up.

She tells him Elsie didn't get a honeymoon.

He doesn't ask who Elsie is, just gives the look and says I don't get you sometimes and then adds: that's part of why I love you.

It's another reason why. Number six is it?

It is five years; five years since Alfred was taken away and Elsie wonders if they will ever have the life she builds inside her head. Alfred's leave was cancelled again and the last letter says the First Battalion have now moved on from Egypt and he makes it all sound so exotic – so romantic, lists of place names, most she has never heard of. He has even been to Bethlehem. She imagines a nativity scene, a star guiding him home. He talks of places Elsie can't even imagine – a far cry from Canning Town with its grey skies, rain, and endless winters.

Please come home to me.

She hears them talk of Nazis more and more in the news.

They have promised me, Elsie, he writes. Promised me leave, write it in that journal of yours: September 4th 1939. We will finally be together, my love.

Blog post: **Structure**

The writer has to work out the very best way to tell a story. She says how there are many ways and it's about finding the right internal structure, dispensing with too much exposition, focussing on the key events, slowly building the tension. But she is sure she has not quite got this story right, it feels too fast, what really happened in those five years? Has she dispensed with them too quickly, not really built the dramatic tension enough? It is as if she has missed out what it was really like for Elsie. It seems implausible, five years; she wishes she knew how to climb inside her head; truly inhabit her, know what she feels. But how can she relate?

Her new husband has spent a day in London. She has found the time to write and yet she misses him. The house is too still. She loves her own space and so does he and yet somehow there is a space that sits and waits to be filled, like an ache.

The dog spends all day staring at the front door.

… and yet Elsie is five years into a marriage, all those anniversaries spent alone. And still she waits as if her whole life, and not just a single day, is on pause, how large is that ache? Large enough to fall inside…? Lose yourself?

She blogs about her novel and a child who went missing the day Kennedy was assassinated and is still missing fifty years on. She adds something about real people, how missing someone is truly the worst feeling of all, and in stories is a motivator of action, the pain drives you: *write how you feel, Donut*… But she deletes it because it feels too personal.

The difference with what happened to her, is her 'missing' person is never coming home. She'd held his hand until it turned cold and she'd said her goodbyes. *Let go* she told him. *Just close your eyes and let go.*

She didn't mean it. Who does?

But Elsie knew her husband was still alive.

Elsie had his letters and not just old ones in a battered shoebox, like the one she has somewhere, more cards than letters, like who writes letters these days? She used to have texts from him, until her phone died.

How did Elsie survive?

Do you stop wondering, stop believing, or do you let love carry you? How fast did those five years seem? The man *she* loved first has been gone more than twelve years but it's hard to feel time as it passes. Hard to quantify. Like trying to hold a bubble in your hand but the edges are too fragile they just… break apart.

It's all relative.

Last year went so fast – they all said it would – planning

a wedding, a perfect day full of perfect moments… but like everything else is soon a memory.

Should she play with the story structure? Should she tell Elsie's story in a different way; in a less chronological way? She writes in her blog how some stories play time backwards and she thinks about that.

What do you think about stories that start at the end? she asks him when he gets in from the gym.

At the end?

Yeah.

So you know the ending first? He had one eye on his mobile phone, buried by Instagram hashtags.

Yeah.

Isn't that giving it away? Would your novel have worked if you'd known what happened to the missing child at the start?

Well yeah… but that's different, and—

Besides, he hadn't even read her novel.

He does not read fiction.

She hears him say you know best, babe. I don't know a single thing about writing stories.

How different they really are. Yet how… similar.

They have both been lost.

He helps people find themselves, better versions of themselves, it's all good but yoga is the best he says. His clients learn to retake their lives. She helps people visit places they have never been. Inhabit characters they have never met; reinvent themselves, just in a different way: it's all about change. Like thermodynamics. Did Elsie change? Was she the person who married Alfred, and what about him?

When someone is separated from their love for so long, won't the reader want to know how it all ends up? If Alfred ever makes it home? If Elsie ever gets her honeymoon?

The writer already knows how it ends of course, she always did.

She fumbles with a black and white photograph she found online and she looks at the faces of a couple taken after the war: the woman is smiling.

She thinks of her story: how did Elsie stay so strong for all those years?

> *I waited because what else was there? They said he was coming home and then he wasn't and then he was and it's all I could do to hold the pieces together and then—*

The writer needs to keep the tension going, so what happened after all that waiting?

> *The Nazis.*
>
> *War broke out and all leave from the British Army was cancelled.*
>
> *Elsie remembers the announcement on the wireless, she remembers clutching his last letter: I promise, this time I'll be home with you, my lovely Elsie. This time...*
>
> *She remembers the Telegram; the news his battalion was to be deployed in the war efforts and God alone knew when he would be home – if he would ever be home. Oh but he would, because... well because he had to be. They needed their honeymoon.*
>
> *It would all be over by Christmas.*
> *Isn't that what they said last time?*

The writer blogs about taking characters to their lowest point and slowly building to the story climax, as if all paths lead to one place, like wise men following a star.

Maybe for Elsie it was the never knowing it would be so long that drove her towards that point; that guided her.

Like writing a novel... if you knew when you started the journey that it would be so hard would you still do it? It's what she asked him last night.

Yes. Of course you would, honey. You can't live without your passion just as I can't live without mine.

Yes... *how right he was.*

I love your passion for everything he says.

Is that seven?

Huh?

She wonders if Elsie coped by thinking this time next month, next year, it would all be over and they could begin their married life. I mean it had to be one day, didn't it?

How strange that good news rides alongside the bad, how life carries on amongst the bombs. The seasons change: Christmases come and go, people die, including her own mother – and Alf is still not home. She spends more and more time with Alf's sister. She is having a baby. Life carries on. What about their babies? They have not even had their honeymoon.

Each rejection is one step closer to success.

She blogged about that once. How small that seems compared to what she is putting Elsie through. England will have been dangerous. Bombs fell from the sky, people died, dogs died, houses were gone, brothers, sons, dads and husbands never came home.

She reads the Telegram again. She has always held the pieces together, stopped the sky from falling. But now she falls to her knees and the sound is like a muffled baby's cry that catches where it forms.

She hears Alf's sister say something, is she okay, what is it? He's not— is he? Like the words are too big to say.

The Telegram slips from her fingers onto the cold stone kitchen floor. The words: Alfred is a prisoner of war.

And now the cold stone floor is covered with pieces of sky.

Blog post: **Horror Stories**

She blogs that stories must live long after you turn the last page. And horror stories in particular will leave images the reader can't shake. She mentions Stephen King, master of storytelling. She loves to write horror but she realises that some horrors are worse than anything in the pages of a Stephen King novel.

She remembers a history class, a potted version of the war in Japan and prisoners who died building the Burma railway; one part of one lesson because there was so much more to say about the Nazis, the Holocaust in Europe. That is another horror story, one she has also written many stories about. But never about Changi, not until now. When she asked at school what it was really like, they said *haven't you watched Tenko?* But it's fiction.

I think it's time to show me.
Show me what it was really like, Alfred...

These past nights her pink cotton pillows have filled up with questions.

But the past is obdurate.

It's something Stephen King says in one of his novels: *his* Kennedy one. It does not give up its secrets easily. And nor does Alfred. But she knows she has to write about Changi; about the Goldfish Parade.

She wonders if Alfred would ever write home to Elsie about what it was really like? But she already knows the answer – it is up to her, the writer, to do that.

At first, the soldiers were told to write of only good things; like playing football with the guards and favours for cigarettes, and sunshine… not the storms.

Bury it all… like the dead. And there were lots of dead – it was a miracle any of them survived.

So… what happened to Alfred?

That is the question that she must resolve; the star all roads lead to – but first she must show the reader what Alfred showed her. It came to her like a dream as she slept, she woke up and the words were there.

I will show only what you need to see, Donut…

Monday, November 30th, 1942

It's the stench that gets you at first: death.

It smothers, clings to everything. In the end you get used to it and how wrong that seems… but you must never write that in a letter. NEVER say that to the ones you love.

Or how you're sick of rice and rotten meat but it's all you have to sustain you on twenty-four hour shifts, sometimes longer, digging until you bleed; laying railway track in all that heat, and sometimes in the middle of a monsoon. And God… the maggots… bloody maggots crawl on the meat, and on your skin, and then there are the flies and the mosquitos.

You know you have malaria again and you feel every weeping pore of your sallow skin and every sinew of muscle, what's left of it. But mustn't tell them at home.

It's not so bad, you write… doing okay… be home soon.

You could drop down right now where so many have, but you won't.

Got to keep fighting.

It's what you tell them – Fred, fellow Londoner from First Battalion, Manchester Reg. Been together from the start – through all of this and you tell him, "You know, Fred, it's about getting back up no matter what the bastards do to you. Be there at Goldfish Parade each night, laugh at them 'cause you survived another day; you're still here no matter what they do. And don't believe a bloody thing they tell you. Your family is still there, it's all lies…"

And him saying, "Yeah, Alf, you're right."

You told Fred the parade is where you march even when you can't stand up. Like a roll call every night. And if you fall you get back up and you keep on getting back up.

"Know what I think about, Alfie, Boy? Home. Me mum and dad…"

"You do that, Fred. Think about what is waiting for you, 'cause that's what's gonna get you out of this."

And then he'd get that glazed look. "But Alf, what if I don't make it?"

"You will."

"But if I don't, you'll go an' see my folks, right? Tell them I tried, that I love 'em, right?"

"Don't talk that way, Fred. We're getting out of here, you, me, Charlie, all of us. Got that?"

"Yeah, but promise me, if I don't make it, Alf, you'll take care of the folks, you'll pass on me message."

"I promise… but you can tell 'em yourself when all this is over."

You think about Elsie, that's what you think about at the Goldfish Parade. Her sweet face, waiting for you.

Elsie.

The world starts and ends with Elsie.

Monday June 7th, 1943

It is the day Fred fell.

It happened as you finished up another section of railway; you heard him cry out, the thud of his fall and then another thud: a boot in his side. It's a sound you're used to.

GET UP, FREDDY BOY!

GET UP, FREDDY!

You had each other's back. You waited for him to get back up. Like all the other times.

GET UP, FRED!

Only this time he never did.

Dead before he hit and left where he fell.

And later, as you march in the Goldfish Parade you have another reason to go on. You'll do it for Fred and one day you'll look his mum and dad in the eyes and tell 'em how brave he was, and how much he loved 'em. How much he wanted to come home.

You have a promise to keep now, Alf.

Friday July 21st, 1944

Malaria. Like a mist descending: delirium.

It makes you think of Fred and of home and of your

mother's cooking... you will your spent legs to keep on marching, round and round you go: but legs are too heavy. So HEAVY.

Stand still, just for a moment. Just for a—

Close your eyes. What do you see? Elsie's sweet sweet face.

Soft bed sheets... honeymoon...
THUD.
GET UP, ALFIE, BOY...
Fred?
GET UP, ALF...
Is that you, Fred?

The last thing you feel is the earth. Hard on fragile bones.

The last thing you hear is Fred. GET UP, ALFIE, BOY...

And the last thing you see is her sweet face.
I'm sorry, Elsie love. I. Am. So. Very. Sorry. I tried.

Blog post: **Endings series {Part 1}: How does it end?**

She writes about sad endings, how readers prefer happy endings; or at the very least give a sad ending hope. But how?

What do you think about stories with sad endings she asks him later as they settle down in front of another Netflix film.

Eh?

What do you think about sad endings?

I thought you said you'd not seen this, not got a sad ending has it, I prefer—

No, I mean stories in general.

Oh.
He smiles.
What?
I love how you ask me and I have no idea what you are even talking about.
Does that make eight reasons why?
I love you just for being you.
Nine. Are we almost there?

Elsie stares at washing on a line and hears the wireless from somewhere deep inside the house. It has been three months since the last letter arrived. It has never been this long. This is her new mantra now... It has never been this long. She watches the light catch in her wedding band. It has never been this long.

How can it be ten years without him?

She doesn't say it out loud but that night she writes in her journal. God, please hear me: Don't let Alfred be dead. Please. Don't. Be. Dead.

Blog post: **Endings series {Part 2}: Like A Sandwich**

It's another post in her series on endings and resolutions, people seem to like it, she gets lots of likes.

Imagine that writing a story is eating a sandwich she says, you need to make it the best sandwich anyone ever ate. Throw in some surprise fillings, to keep them enjoying it and make them love it to the very last bite. Then… make it live long after; make them keep on eating it again and again in their head.

Babe, only you can make a writer's blog about food he says as he sits there tying the shoelaces of his latest retro New Balance trainers, getting ready to teach his yoga class. She has been mumbling as she reads her post back.

It's just a metaphor she says.

I don't even know what a metaphor is.

Of course you do.

I don't he laughs, I'm not like you, you're academic, I'm—

Okay alone, stronger together.

It's when something is something else.

Eh? He looks confused. Shakes his head. Whatever you say, babe. You're an angel.

She laughs.

What?

Nothing.

Then he stands up and leans in for a kiss. Let's book the honeymoon when I get home. You've had that passport two weeks.

Yes. Now go, I need to finish my story...

The day starts with the thing; the thing she has imagined and reimagined over and over.

A Telegram.

Blog post: <u>Endings series {Part 3}</u>: Keep the tension going to the very end

Writers have a tendency to gallop to the finish line, but say it slowly, choose your words carefully.

Elsie stands and reads the words again. She cries out.

Blog Post: <u>Endings series {Part 4}</u>: The final twist

Her hands hover over the keys, wedding band glinting in the sunshine from the office window. She writes how the new story is finally finished and how for the first time this one is not really fiction; it's more personal than that. She wonders if she should tell them why...

Propped against the black computer tower on her desk

is a black and white photograph; the one she printed off the internet… the couple. Who can believe someone is selling a photograph of her grandparents on eBay… and for £99? It is from a newspaper archive (a job lot apparently) and there is a photo of the inscription on the back which she has also printed. It reads:

December 27th, 1945…

Honeymoon After Twelve Years of Marriage

Lance-Corporal and Mrs Alfred Sheldrake of Beresford Gardens, Chadwell Heath, London, spent a happy Christmas enjoying their delayed honeymoon. A few hours after their wedding in 1933, the army intervened and has kept Lance-Corporal Sheldrake on the move all over the world ever since. He recently came home from Singapore where he had been a prisoner of war.

Next to the photographs is another; this one a real photograph and not just a print-out – of a slender attractive young woman in a long black coat, and a black hat tilted on her head, dark curls beneath it. Her mum gave it to her when she'd shown her what she'd found on eBay.

I remember the press taking that photo of them, her mum had said, I might even have the article… so for goodness sake don't buy it!

No way. It's outrageous she said.

You look like her he says when she shows him the photo. Even that coat and definitely the hat. You look so much alike.

Really? She only realised that when she was getting her

hair done on her wedding day. For a moment she saw her face; in her reflection. Even if it has been forty years since she died. She always knew her brother looked like Alf, it's uncanny how much... but her? He sees it too?

It gives her an idea for a new blog post, she scribbles it in her notebook under the other idea: *Life is stranger than fiction.* This one simply says: *Does history repeat?*

So this is the story you were writing? he says, watching her, sipping his coffee saying how his class was full this morning. This is Alfred and Elsie?

Yeah. I asked my grandad to show me what it is like being in that place, but he wouldn't tell me at first, I mean they used to ask him to sell his story to the newspapers Mum said. But he would never talk about it. Took it to his grave. So I begged him... and... it's like he whispered it to me in a dream.

He reaches for her hand.

It was supposed to be a horror story. I wanted the world to know what he survived, how he still got back up even with malaria and how, of his battalion, less than a third made it home. He was one of the ones who boosted everyone else's morale, kept them all going. I didn't include the part about how, for the rest of his life, he would never touch rice, or drive Japanese cars... how Mum would come home from school and find him sleeping on the hard wooden floors in the hallway. PTSD I guess, only they didn't have a fancy name for it then. And one time he got done for contempt of court. He was such a placid man. When he was a chauffeur, a bus went into him, entirely the bus driver's fault, but it went to court. It was a case he should have won, he so easily *would have* won... that's why he represented himself... only the bus driver's lawyer was Japanese. Swords at dawn. He lost it, flipped out.

I mean, he knew they weren't all the same, he always

knew that... but I guess sometimes the line between 'then' and 'now' gets blurred.

She thinks how they will never really know the true horror of it.

She feels his stare as she gazes at the photograph of her grandparents: Alf sat at a piano, Elsie standing at his side looking at him, smiling.

He told me to make it a story about love, not horror.

I like that, her husband tells her.

That I had to tell *her* story, not his. How she waited all those years. Twelve. A similar amount of time since my Lee died of cancer. Hard to measure, quantify...

She felt the warmth of his fingers as they entwined with hers.

But I had to tell some of his story to tell hers.

He nods.

It must have been... I mean we couldn't even imagine what he went through in that place. I had to write it, but I embellished a bit, I thought I'd made up the part about 'Fred' (only I called him Tom at first) and the promise part, fictional license but you know... when I told Mum she said that really happened, only his name was Fred and her twin brother (who died as a baby) was named after him. Grandad always stayed in touch with his family and he did go to them when he came back, so it seems there *was* a promise and he did keep it.

She gets goose bumps whenever she thinks about that. She looks at her new hubby...

But he didn't show me the real horror. Not the torture or—

Maybe you didn't need that for your story to work.

Yeah but—

He was protecting you, babe.

You think? And you believe me when I say it was like he spoke to me?

Yes.

And that I think somehow he led me to the photo on eBay too, like a serendipitous wrong click on Google and there it was. He made me see the real story he wanted told. The headline on the back is the real story, better than anything I could have made up.

Come here. He kisses her softly on the lips. Of course I believe you. It's just energy and theirs is around us, watching over us, they saw the wedding, they see it all.

I hope so.

She thinks about her brother, his new wife, the baby on the way.

Should I blog about the real story?

Up to you, babe... but isn't it like putting your whole life out there, like we're all in some kind of giant goldfish bowl with everyone looking in?

When he said that she studied his serious expression.

What?

Nothing.

Does the world have to see and know *everything?*

She leans in to press her lips to his cheek.

What was that for?

You're right – just show them what they need to see.

Come on – let's book the honeymoon.

She steals another glance at the photograph. *Thank you for telling me your story. Love overcomes evil – it had to be about love.*

And then she thinks about the other thing her mum'd said, how Elsie was pregnant with her and her twin brother when the photograph was taken for the newspaper. They didn't hang about; nor did her brother and his wife.

Her fingers lightly dance across the image.

So, looks like they got their happy ending she says. If they hadn't, if he'd died in Changi, there would be no story…

Why not? It would just have had a different ending. A sad one...

No, there would be no story...

He looks deep into her eyes. No?

Because there would be no me.

He seems to think about that before he says, know why I love you?

Because I say weird things like that?

No.

The tenth reason?

If you say so.

Go on then...

Because you're my happy ending, no matter what life throws at us.

To anyone else it's a tiny moment that will pass unnoticed. Like something out of a cheesy Hallmark movie... but she knows with him it's real, it's the way he is with her, the way she is with him: *okay alone, stronger together... greater than the sum of all parts...* like Alfred and Elsie. Love is real. Love is the star that brings wise men home.

And you're my happy ending she says. Now come on let's get this bloody honeymoon booked!

About this story
I wanted to finish the collection with my most recent work. I have to tell you of all the stories in this collection this is the *most* personal. I have never written a story directly about me before and this *is* a true story. I do write a blog about writing, I did get married in January after losing my *first* true love to cancer and my grandad was in Changi. I have always wanted to write something about him – and it is true that he would never talk about what happened in Singapore. He died in 1978 when I was just nine years old so I never got the chance to ask him myself – until now. Because yes – I *did* ask him to help me and I believe he did lead me to the photograph pictured below and inspired me to write a story about love – not horror. It had to be about love. Everything is about love.

That is why I have dedicated this collection to all my grandparents – but in particular *this story* to Alfred and Elsie Sheldrake. Elsie is also on the cover of this book in the other photograph that is referenced in this story.

Alfred and Elsie Sheldrake: my grandparents.
Photograph taken in 1945.

About the Author

Debz Hobbs-Wyatt lives on Canvey Island in Essex with her husband, cocker spaniel and two cats. She is a full-time writer and editor and has an MA in Creative Writing from Bangor University. She gave up her day job as a scientist to pursue her writing career in 2010.

She has a writing blog where she talks about all things *writerly* and calls herself 'Writerly Debz' – the official WordzNerd. Link: www.wordznerd.wordpress.com

She edits and mentors clients of all levels: from full manuscript appraisals to final proofreads. She also does manuscript appraisals for Cornerstones Literary Consultancy. Check out her website here: www.debzhobbs-wyatt.co.uk

Her debut novel *While No One Was Watching* was published in 2013 by Parthian Books to some great reviews. She has a few novels in various stages of completion and hopes to have a new novel out very soon. Do check out her pages for news.

www.facebook.com/DebzHobbsWyattAuthor
@WriterDebz (Instagram)
@DebzHobbsWyatt (Twitter)

Debz says writing for a living isn't about the money or the fame – writing is a passion. If you have it, you can't ignore it. If those other things come as reward for the hard work – then it's a beautiful bonus. But, the most important thing is doing what you love every day; that is the greatest blessing of all.

Other Publications by Debz Hobbs-Wyatt

While No One was Watching

by Debz Hobbs-Wyatt

The US President, John F Kennedy, is assassinated as his motorcade hits town, watched by crowds of spectators and the world s media. Watching too from the grassy knoll nearby is a young mother who, in the confusion, lets go of her daughter's hand. When she turns around the little girl has vanished.

Fifty years later, when everyone remembers what they were doing at that moment in history, she is still missing. Who will remember her? Local hack Gary Blanchet, inspired by the mother's story, joins forces with former police psychic Lydia Collins to seek answers. They re-examine the evidence from that day, but this time they re not looking for a man in a crowd with a gun; they are looking for little Eleanor Boone.

Gone, while no one was watching? Maybe someone was.

Order from Amazon:

Paperback: ISBN 978-1-908946-32-4
eBook: ASIN B00FWRJ80O

Other Publications by Bridge House

Links

by Dianne Stadhams

LINKS – sometimes random, many times unplanned, often with far reaching consequences, always shaping our journey from cradle to grave – the stuff of life.

Just how do Atta Gatta the child-eating crocodile, Scheherazade the pantomime star and Judy the stammering Goth strategically connect characters across the globe?

Enjoy this trilogy of inter-linked short stories that will make you smile and squirm as they raise questions about the needs and challenges of our contemporary world.

Order from Amazon:

Paperback: ISBN 978-1-907335-63-1
eBook: ISBN 978-1-907335-64-8

The Art of Losing

by Paul Williams

In this internationally-acclaimed collection of contemporary literary fiction stories by Paul Williams we are invited to appreciate what it means to master the art of losing – to let go of things both big and small – whether it be dreams, or love, or houses, or whole continents. Told with wit, humour and pathos, the stories reveal the unexpected narratives that often flow beneath the surface of contemporary lives.

The twenty stories lurch from continent to continent across Australia, Europe and South Africa, from child to teen to adult, from past to present, from war to peace, from me to you.

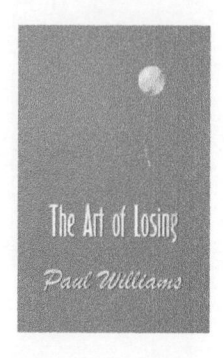

Order from Amazon:

Paperback: ISBN 978-1-907335-61-7
eBook: ISBN 978-1-907335-52-5

Keepsake

by Jenny Palmer

Keepsake and Other Stories is an anthology of short stories by one of the growing number of brave women writers. Jenny Palmer brings us stories of otherness, witchcraft and magic close to home and further afield within Europe. We meet all sorts of characters: those who rely on guard dogs, those who shun social media and those who are obsessed. We even meet a Neanderthal man. There are paranormal stories, a story of bad neighbours, and a story of redundancy. And many more. All to be enjoyed.

"Jenny is totally in control of her stories. They are memorable and perfectly crafted." (*Amazon*)

Order from Amazon:
Paperback: ISBN 978-1-907335-57-0
eBook: ISBN 978-1-907335-58-7

Milton Keynes UK
Ingram Content Group UK Ltd.
UKHW010050250124
436604UK00003B/21

9 781907 335693